Logan,

Thanks, and I mean it,
for all the kind words, Hope
you enjoy these and, more

important, that we'll get this
summer, a few chances to talk

All the best

Mark

Bull

Mark Sinnett

a misFit
book

INSOMNIAC PRESS

Edited by Michael Holmes/a misFit book
Copy edited by Lloyd Davis & Liz Thorpe
Designed by Mike O'Connor

Canadian Cataloguing in Publication Data

Sinnett, Mark, 1963-
     Bull

ISBN 1-895837-27-8

I. Title.

PS8587.I563B84 1998   C813'.54   C98-930406-X
PR9199.3.S56B84 1998

A few of the stories, in different forms, have appeared before. "Dope" and "Moth" were in *blood and aphorisms*, "Africa" was in *The New Quarterly*, and "The Green Bug" appeared in *The Nashwaak Review*. Cheers to the editors.

The publisher gratefully acknowledges the support of the Ontario Arts Council.

The author also received some life-support from the Ontario Arts Council. Beautiful stuff.

Printed and bound in Canada

Insomniac Press, 393 Shaw Street,
Toronto, Ontario, Canada, M6J 2X4
www.insomniacpress.com

For my family, here and there.
And in memory of my grandmother,
Dorothy Emma Sinnett (1909-1997).

Yes, it struck her now that this whole business of the bull was like a life; the important birth, the fair chance, the tentative, then assured, then half-despairing circulations of the ring, an obstacle negotiated — a feat improperly recognised — boredom, resignation, collapse: then another, more convulsive birth, a new start; the circumspect endeavours to obtain one's bearings in a world now frankly hostile, the apparent but deceptive encouragement of one's judges, half of whom were asleep, the swervings into the beginnings of disaster because of that same negligible obstacle one had surely taken before at a stride, the final enmeshment in the toils of enemies one was never quite certain weren't friends more clumsy than actively ill-disposed, followed by disaster, capitulation, disintegration...
    —Malcolm Lowry

We look almost happy in the sun, while we bleed to death
        from wounds we don't know about.
    —Tomas Tranströmer (tr. Don Coles)

I tell you all my secrets
but I lie about my past.
    —Tom Waits

Contents

Acknowledgements

For reading bits and pieces, lending a hand, an ear, I am grateful to Mary Cameron, Mike Epplett, Steve Heighton, Lisu Hill, Jane Lafarga, Ryan Land, Chris Miner, Samantha Mussells, Colin Turcotte and Daniel Woods. Special thanks to my editor, Michael Holmes.

Dope

Pitbull puppies, six females.
12" South American Alligator w/
tank. Call 584-4341. Leave message.

I read that classified ad to Jenny and she thinks it's the funniest
thing she's ever heard.

"Can you imagine what those people look like?" She puts her
hands on her hips and stares into space, imagining them. Me, I
check out Jenny's body. We still haven't been together that
long, certainly not long enough for me to take her physique for
granted. That'll come. I know myself pretty well, so I take every
advantage. Recognize your limitations is what I say.

"Shit!" Jenny says. "I bet they live in the north end. You
think?"

I shrug, tell her maybe it's just some kids from the university
fooling around.

"And I bet the police call them," Jenny says confidently,
more to herself than to me. She nods fiercely, as if a revelation,
a great religious truth, has just transported her to a higher con-
sciousness. "Yeah, to get the address, you know? God, anyone
selling pitbulls and crocodiles has got to be selling dope, fenc-
ing stereos too. No way one happens without the other."

"So you figure some cop reads the classifieds every day?"

"I think they call all the escort agencies," Jenny says, collapsing onto the couch. "And send the undercovers on dates to see what's really for sale."

She wiggles her toes at me. The nails are a vivid red — scarlet — and I've got to admit it's a turn-on. At first, you think, Christ, that's tacky; but now I love them. It's just one of those details. You've got no idea how you're going to react.

A while later we're sipping a couple of beers, watching TV. Jenny looks over and says, "Call."

I know exactly what she means but I play ignorant, squint at her.

"Go on, call them. Make like you're interested in one of the puppies."

I squirm a bit. It's a funny idea, sure, but it makes me uncomfortable. I'm not into taking the mickey the way Jenny is. Hell, we'll go out some nights and she's nudging me, pointing out what she calls *fashion disasters*, and bouncing up and down when a fight breaks out. She absolutely loves the misery of a falling-down drunk. There's a sadistic streak in her, a wide swath of cruelty.

Anyhow, ten minutes of goading and I'm on the phone, listening to the ring and wondering what kind of civilized home I've just invaded. Jenny leans forward, elbows on her knees. She pushes her hair behind her ears so she won't miss anything. Expectant is how she looks. But I just get the answering machine and hang up, a bit relieved.

"Leave a message," Jenny says, disappointed, pouting. "Call back and ask them how big they expect the croc to get."

"Alligator," I correct her, worried it's this slapdash attention to detail that's going to get us in trouble.

"Whatever. Ask them how big it'll get."

I ask her to place the call. I flatter her, say she's funnier than I am. "And sweeter, too. If it gets nasty you'll straighten it out better than I would."

When she agrees, I'm shocked. "Okay, here, swap seats," she says.

I watch her mouth a few words, rehearsing. But then, right when she expects the tape to roll, someone picks up.

"Uh, hello there," she starts, blushing so much it complements, to my mind, her nail polish. But I can see the wheels are still turning, Plan B coming around. Now it's me who assumes the pose: hunched forward, all ears.

"I'm calling about the puppies," she says. "*And* the alligator, actually. How much do you want for all of it?" She nods slowly. "Yes. That's right, the whole kit and caboodle."

I hold my breath.

"They've had all their shots, have they?" Jenny inquires. "What about the alligator? Oh, I don't know, malaria, distemper, rabies."

She winks at me, nods some more. I can hear the tinny sounds of a voice, a man.

Jenny says, "No, I really don't think we'd be interested in the aquarium. No. My husband says we can just use the bathtub. Yes, I think he's crazy too, but... What do they eat, by the way? Hmm. Will it get along with the dogs? Oh, don't even answer that. If it doesn't, we'll just get some shoes made."

I hear the guy getting excited.

"No, not at all," Jenny says, "I'm quite serious."

But whoever she's tormenting doesn't buy it. He starts yelling. I feel vulnerable and wonder if there's anything he can do to us. I get half-way off my chair, tug at Jenny's arm. All of a sudden I'm having real doubts about my relationship with her, wondering what it would take in the way of physical pain or legal proceedings before I ratted her out. Jenny pulls free, shushes me, and I jump up and mute the television, as if that might give us away.

"How about drugs?" Jenny says. "Could we pick up some coke, a couple of grams maybe, when we collect the animals? Be damn nice of you to just throw that in gratis since we're taking the whole menagerie. And your TV. You got a nice Sony for us?"

I catch the barrage of abuse the guy levels at Jenny. Slut,

bitch, the usual. Then Jenny drowns it out with laughter. She tips back in her chair, slaps at her leg.

"Good one," she hoots. Pretty soon her eyes are watering she's laughing so hard. And then suddenly, like her power was cut off, she stops, says, "Okay, bye," and hangs up. Nice as pie again. The demure schoolgirl. Legs together, fiddling with her hair, clearing her throat.

"Great stuff," I tell her, not as amused, as comfortable, as I want to be. "Really funny."

Five minutes later our phone rings, louder than it ever has before, and we have one of those *Get it; No, you get it* conversations before the machine picks up. It's the guy. Has to be. First he just snorts, pleased with himself. Then:

"Yeah, that's your voice all right, Honey. Think it's funny, do you? Well, I'll show you funny. I'm gonna go through the phone book, number by number, until I come up with your address. I don't care how damn long it takes. Then we'll see..."

He starts to chuckle, seems to really get into it, and keeps it up, forces it out, until the tape cuts him off.

For a second neither of us moves. Then Jenny leaps up and dashes to the kitchen like she smells something burning. When she comes back it's with the phone book in one hand, a bottle of Cuervo and two glasses in the other. She pours two large shots, half fills the glasses. Then she sits back, smug-looking. "Let's see," she says, flipping pages.

By now I'm kind of frantic. My attention darts everywhere: to the muted television, the front door, the telephone. It always settles, though, on Jenny.

"You think he was serious?" I ask. "Do you?"

Jenny looks at me as if she's just realized I'm an idiot, a complete moron, and then she goes back to the directory.

"Hah!" She jabs triumphantly at the open page.

"Just tell me," I say.

"No address, just our phone number."

I'm relieved, I feel my body relax, stomach muscles in partic-ular, but I remind her, "And a name, right?"

She peers down at the line, blinks. "Oh yeah. Shit."

She swirls the tequila, dabs a finger into it. Takes a drink and holds the fiery liquid in her mouth a while before she swallows. "Still," she muses finally, "it's your name, right? Not mine."

The Cost of Lamb

"Ahh, Christmas Eve," I say out loud, embarrassing myself. I whistle a few shrill, hasty notes. But the truth is, I'm getting off on the dreary romance of being alone. Vicky's gone to Windsor to see her parents. I was supposed to tag along, then last minute her mum and dad decided Georgia, our dog, couldn't come, and of course all the kennels were booked solid. So instead of saying, *Sorry, won't be able to make it this year*, we separated. We've been together, what, eight years? And it's always the same: we think of some reason why our parents would be devastated without our presence. It's bullshit. We've got to grow up and do our own thing is what I think.

I decant some Scotch into a favourite tumbler. It's just a juice glass — plain, utilitarian. But I was once served some single malt this way at a Tex-Mex joint in Toronto. And it makes you think you're getting a lot for your money. A trick glass, I guess, and strangely, intoxicatingly sophisticated in the hand. It took me months to find some exactly the same, searching all the fancy glassware places. Finally I tracked them down in a dollar store next to Zellers, four for a buck. Anyway, I pour myself a double, which means damn near two-thirds of a glass. Then I lie back on the couch, start poking randomly at the remote.

I try to come up with a song, a "My baby left me and it's snowing outside" kind of thing, but I'm lousy with lyrics. I can be sitting in a bar telling some guy how much I love an album, how it's changed my life, and he'll say, "Well, how does it go?" And when that happens it's like I'm a parrot and someone's thrown a blanket over my cage. So I lie there struck dumb, and flick to a movie on TVO. Audrey Hepburn is booting around France in a convertible, with a guy it takes me twenty minutes to identify as Albert Finney. I whistle a nonsense tune, make up my own words, but nothing repeatable, nothing memorable. Georgia is curled asleep at my feet. I feel like the lord of the manor.

Vicky must have arrived by now. It's gone eight o'clock; she left at three thirty. I hope the drive was okay; there are always so many people rushing home on the 24th. For a morbid instant I see her crashing, being run into a ditch, the icy 401 littered with Christmas presents. I identify a half-unwrapped food processor, a sea-green sweater tumbling through the gravel, six golf balls still in their black lacquered box. Blood congealing over the road like old cranberry sauce. Festive stuff.

I pilfer a slice of Christmas cake from the kitchen, suck on the marzipan, whittle it down. Vicky would be pissed. She's got this thing about not indulging until the morning of the 25th. That means we can't eat any of the holiday food, or crack open the expensive liqueurs. All we do early is stand a tree laden with ribbons, hand-blown glittery orbs, in the front window. It's important, apparently, that we put on a decadent show for the neighbours but deprive ourselves of everything. I feel like a Buddhist monk, an ascetic sorely tempted by Christian baubles. I decide to lie, to tell her I cut into the cake at breakfast. Or, if she's late getting back, I'll make it lunch. Say I was excited.

Our cat creeps into the living room. Lenny never forgave us for getting a dog. Scared shitless he is. Comes up those stairs like a soldier scouting enemy territory. He usually grabs a few mouthfuls of food, slurps some water and then he's gone again. We should put a bowl down there for him, I suppose, but Vicky hopes this little cruelty of ours will eventually pay off. *I want everyone to get along*, she says, *not to disappear all the time.* Sweet.

I check the time again: nine-thirty. Vicky will be settled around the family tree. My whisky is almost done and I try to picture the bottle, how much is left in it. "Lenny," I say. "Lenny." I drop an arm to the floor and scratch at the carpet. I like Lenny, he's a cool cat. But it looks like he's in a bad way tonight. He's hunched over and trembling like an old man with one of those degenerative diseases that leaves you an empty nervous shell, a stiff husk of twitches and spasms.

I slide forwards off the couch and Georgia startles awake. I feel like a zookeeper sometimes. I move in to scoop Lenny up, but I'm scared of hurting him so I fetch a couple ounces of water in a tiny Japanese teacup instead. The cat's tongue drops to the water, hangs there like a towel he hopes will absorb moisture. It's fascinating. I lay on my chest and watch. I note also that Finney is being a real bastard to Hepburn, throwing the car all over the road. I can smell whiskey and raisins on my fingers. Then blood begins to dribble, trickle over Lenny's black lips and that's it, I've had enough. This is no curiosity any more. Fuck, I think. Fuck fuck fuck.

The woman at the answering service tells me the vet is reluctant to go into the office. "Can't it wait until Boxing Day?" she asks. When I don't respond she adds: "Or at least until he's done the gift thing with the kids tomorrow. Say eleven, eleven-thirty?" She's nice about it, though. You can tell that she wants me to understand she's only the messenger.

So I'm nice back, but firm. "Tell the doctor I think the cat's dying. Have you got him on another line?"

"No. I'll have to call him again. I hope he picks up."

"If he doesn't, I want his address."

I think this freaks her out a bit because two minutes later she calls back. "The vet will be at the office in half an hour," she says.

I lift Lenny delicately into a banana box, wrap him in a burgundy towel. The phone rings yet again and I decide that if it's the vet, hoping to do a consultation from the comfort of his home, to talk me through some wildly complicated feline surgery, I'm going to lose it.

"Guess what. I'm coming home!" It's Vicky.

"Hilarious. Very funny."

"No really, I got kicked out."

I don't believe her.

"Seriously. I'm at Taco Bell. I'll be home really late, but we're going to get Christmas together. That's good, isn't it?"

"Of course it is. But your parents turfed you?"

"I told Susan to go to hell."

"Well, that would do it."

"Dad said I could apologize or pack my bags."

"And they actually let you go. Wow, that's pretty cold."

I ask if she's sure she's doing the right thing. After all, this isn't the same heaven-on-earth she left. Lenny's her favourite. Some days she likes him more than me. A lot more.

Vicky gets defensive, worried that I don't want her around, so I tell her, "Hey, slow down, hold your horses. It's a long drive, that's all. If you're okay to do it, if you haven't been drinking, then great, I'm thrilled. Honest. I..."

But she interrupts me: "Oh God, you should see these two girls who just went by. Real goth types, you know? Torn fishnets, white faces. Wow, beautiful."

Her voice is oddly muffled and I'd bet anything she's got a burrito in her free hand, hot sauce dripping onto the tile floor. Vicky is a sucker for those things. A visit to Taco Bell is pretty much the highlight of a trip home, next to seeing her little brother. There's a silence, and I assume she's watching the two punks disappear into the can. Then she wants to know, "So, will you wait up for me?"

"Of course. I'm too excited to sleep now."

"Because of my arrival, or Santa's?"

We laugh together and when I hang up I'm relieved by that final bit of levity. She'll hit the highway feeling good about us. She'll pay attention to the road.

The vet, Davies, has called in an assistant to help out. I guess he didn't know what to expect. Or maybe he needs her to turn on the computer for him, or the lights. Some smart people are like that. Still, I'm not complaining. This girl is pretty and fawns over Lenny, repeatedly pushing her hair back so it doesn't fall over the cat. Beautiful neck she has too. Shit, I'm such a bastard sometimes. But it's okay, because when she looks up she gets a strong whiff of whisky and her concerned smile dissolves into straight lines, pursed unfriendly lips. Her nose twitches and wrinkles.

The doctor waves me into an examination room. "Let's take a look at what we have here."

The line spills out of him reflexively. I don't suppose he even hears himself. He extracts Lenny from the box, places the animal on a narrow metal table that protrudes from the wall like an ironing board, then stands back and moves a hand up to his chin. It looks practiced more than truly thoughtful, and I wonder if I like this guy very much. Lenny crouches over his own smeared reflection, an emaciated sphinx. The tip of his tongue is a pink button. He vibrates slightly as well, foul breath rattling out. My mother, I realize, sounded a lot like this when she got pneumonia. They gave her pure oxygen mixed with something to open up her airways, inflate the thousand little sacs in her lungs. Every few seconds her eyes rolled back in her head as she fought the gas. Later she claimed to have talked to her dead mother about the soaring cost of lamb in a dank room filled with Johnny Mathis music.

Davies ends his contemplation. He grasps Lenny by the scruff of the neck and with his other hand rolls back the cat's top lip. A strangled "Ahhggh," escapes him and he steps reflexively back from the table. He's immediately embarrassed by his reaction. "Do you smell that? There's pus in there."

I'm half amused. It's like Davies expected a full set of pearly whites, which is ridiculous. But I also sense an accusation.

"He's had teeth problems before," I say. "You did some surgery on him. I don't know if you remember."

Davies lays his hands on the cat again, pushes at the internal organs in a way that makes me queasy. A delicate thread of pink spit descends from Lenny's mouth, approaches the metal table.

"Is it his kidneys?" I ask. "Because the same thing happened to my sister's Siamese."

"Could very well be. Here, let me show you." For a nauseating instant I think he's going to have me feel Lenny's insides, but the doctor extracts a pen from his chest pocket and draws on a scratch pad. He produces a kidney shape on the lemon paper. There is a smear of Lenny's blood on his thumbnail. "This is how a healthy kidney looks. Sort of like a bean."

"And sort of like a swimming pool," I suggest.

"Exactly." He points the pen and his bloody thumb at me. "But this is how Lenny's kidneys look."

The blue ink line curls around on the paper.

"One of them," he explains, "is almost completely round. The other is swollen at one end."

I drift away, don't hear him any more.

It's always something. Sometimes a litany of things. Right now, for instance, there's a hard, granular lump between two toes on my right foot. Probably just my boot rubbing, a worry spot. Trouble is, another one appeared a few days ago at the base of my penis. From the zipper maybe. It's that or it's skin cancer, or syphilis. Half a lifetime ago I necked backstage with a stripper. There was a cheap crystal dish of scarlet potpourri. And now, in this white, stainless steel operating room, I smell that potpourri again, its thick, cloying scent catching in my throat. My mouth is bone dry; I'm a little light-headed. Lenny is vibrating like a macabre wind-up toy. "Is he cold, you think?"

The vet shakes his head. "But he's going to fall off that table if we don't move him." He places the cat on the floor in the centre of the room. Lenny seems swamped, rendered insignificant by the empty space.

I think about Vicky, how far along the highway she must be. I hear the road noise, see the headlights illuminating fifty yards ahead, sense the rush of a transport truck coming alongside.

"The long and the short of it," Dr. Davies says, "is that you have a choice to make. We can put the cat on an IV, give him fluids and antibiotics, hope for some miraculous turnaround... or, we can put him to sleep. It doesn't look good, but it's up to you. We can try. We're more than willing to try."

He's writing all over Lenny's chart, but near the bottom of the page he stops, looks at me expectantly, as if he has to check one of two boxes. I shrug, try to buy a few seconds. I feel like I'm on a game show.

"I don't think I like playing God."

Dr. Davies smiles benignly, blandly, but doesn't respond. He's trying to look sympathetic. He starts to cross his arms but changes his mind. He wants to look open, receptive to my questions. You would think he'd have stock lines for a time like this, some platitudes. It's Christmas Eve, for Christ's sake; that should give him a few ideas.

"So the chances of his recovering to the point where he's not in pain are pretty slim," I try.

He nods. "Lenny might die overnight, whatever you decide. Then again, we can hook him up and he might improve. The fluids alone would probably make him perk up. But then, he might expire when we stopped the IV."

Like milk, I think. *Expire*. Like milk.

"Even if he makes it, Lenny will require some real careful management for the rest of his days, which are unlikely to add up to more than a year."

"So if I hear you right ..."

"It's a hard call."

He checks his watch. I'm infuriated, but I understand his motive enough not to say anything. My thoughts have been elsewhere too, wondering how I'm going to break the news to Vicky. There are only a couple more oblivious hours in her future — Christmas carols on the radio — and then she'll have to face this. I smell bleach, and out in the waiting room the radio gets turned on. Some noisy pop filters through the door.

"Okay, do it." And instantly he's gone, muttering something about permission slips. I glance at the cat's chart, see *renal failure* ticked off from a long list of ailments. I stroke Lenny's head, think about talking. I try to remember some poetry, but it's not going to happen.

"Bon voyage," I say weakly, feeling like a complete asshole. Lenny's breath is a sewer beneath me.

Davies returns and says the file's in Vicky's name but they'll let me sign for it anyway. I scrawl something illegible across the paper.

"You want a few minutes?"

"I think we've had those." I'm reeling now, aghast at what I've done, what I've been forced into.

"Okay Lenny, we're going to make you feel better," Davies coos, scooping up the cat. Lenny drapes like a mink horseshoe, a magnet, over his hand. "You don't want the body, do you? Some people like to take them home."

"What?" I say, astonished, my brain sluggish, not working properly.

"Most people bury the animal in a favourite place, but I suppose the odd one gets..."

"No! Thanks." I feel heartless so I add, "Ground's pretty hard right now."

"It *is* more popular in the summer," Davies agrees. "Okay then. You can settle up at the front."

When I've drained the whisky, I drink gin and lemonade till I'm good and drunk. All the while I'm berating myself for not keeping my wits about me. Vicky's going to want an audience. I watch a few minutes of *It's a Wonderful Life* but decide I need something in colour. There's an old British sitcom on *Bravo!* and I chuckle along grimly with that for a while. Vicky hates this show, says its cruel but can't explain why. Whenever it comes on she goes upstairs and reads, or talks me into changing the channel. Once, they had a mini-festival and played four episodes in a row. Vicky had to leave the house. Said she just walked around and around, couldn't get their stupid lives out of her head. We had an awful argument when she got back. It blew up into something that lasted for days. I scanned the classifieds for apartments I could afford, started wondering about life without her.

She should be walking in the door any time now. Fact is, I'm surprised she's not already here. I feel something grey blooming in my stomach: fear, apprehension, half a bottle of Scotch mixing poorly with the gin.

At four in the morning she still hasn't arrived. I wrap a couple of presents, arrange them around the tree. Some perfume, a first book of photographs by a friend of ours. A few hard-core carollers are wandering the street. It's cold in the house so I turn up the heat, then find the news channel on the TV. The first thing I notice is how absolutely everything on the news is presented in the past tense. *This happened early this morning*, the anchor says grimly, clearing his throat. *Police were on the scene quickly.* I turn the television off, stare blankly at the grey-green screen. It's a minute or two before what I'm looking at registers. It's writing. Vicky must have run a finger mischievously through the thick dust that always collects on the set. *Hi there!* it says, clear as day.

Salt and Pepper

All night it's been the same: Molson Export and Canadian, rum and Coke, rye and ginger. But then some chick made up to look like Courtney Love (the buzz is she's sleeping with the lead singer from tonight's band, taking him for as much coke as she can shovel up her flared equine nostrils with one of those tiny-headed spoons they hand out at McDonald's) wants a vodka crantini. "Lemon slice, please," she orders, snooty as all get out when I deliver the glass naked. She works the room back and forth like she's the ghost of Lady Di — punk royalty — as if that sweet red glassful is the height of elegance. Her brother's the bass player and I know for a fact he's been shooting junk down in the can. Right now he's nodding off at the end of the bar: "He's meditatin'," the drummer explains, "jus' runnin through his moves, ya know?"

"Yeah, I know," I say, nodding. "Don't kid yourself, mate. I know all right."

By twelve-thirty they've only done one frantic twenty-minute set. It wasn't bad, actually, I could use the beat to push myself. And I'm making good money considering this is a room full of headbangers. It's like the drugs make them generous despite their cheap bastardy natures.

When I put glasses in the washer I notice nearly every straw I dump has a scarlet ring of lipstick near the top. Something about it seems obscene, but I can't put my finger on what childhood trauma might be making me feel that way. There's a pain in my chest too, and it moves into my arms whenever I take a deep breath. I know it's either indigestion or a coronary, the embarrassingly banal or the fatal (ain't that a grand predicament), and for fifteen minutes I shuffle around in front of the beer fridges paying way too much attention to my own body. I fuck up a few drinks and suddenly the owner's sticking his shiny pate through the hatch window from the kitchen, wanting to know whether I'm accepting dope as tips.

Some git slithers up to the bar in a too-small Iggy T-shirt, pierced belly, lip, eyebrow. On a chick that can look good, especially the navel thing — I don't mind admitting I find it very, very attractive — but on this geek I don't know. Looks like one of those guys who still needs string tying his mittens together, the type who'll do anything to be part of the crowd. "Salt and pepper chips," he says.

"You mean salt and vinegar," I tell him. He looks at me all mystified like I'm speaking Latin. I explain it to him. "You said salt and pepper, that's all. No biggie."

He peers vacantly at the liqueurs lined up behind me and does a weird thing with his tongue. I don't actually see the muscle but it looks like a mouse is trying to escape his mouth: a lump appears on one cheek and then darts to the other side. I'm thinking, *What's your fucking problem?* when he says, "Well, give me a regular bag and the pepper shaker then, if you don't got what I want."

I laugh, or rather a laugh escapes me, and I put a hand up to my mouth in what is probably a pretty effeminate gesture. Courtney Love is watching us like it's TV, sucking cranberry against gravity; her white straw turns pink. She raises her eyebrows, which I bet are the only naturally coloured hairs on her body, though I suppose you'd have to ask the singer to be sure. Anyway, I watch this guy rip open the packet and go absolutely apeshit with the pepper shaker. I mean, I know he's trying to make a point here, save face or something, but Jesus, those chips look like you dragged them though old kitty litter.

"You mind if I try one of those?" I ask, and of course he's Mr. Generosity then, can't wait to give them away.

"Have another," he says.

"No, thanks," I tell him. The damn thing has nearly burned a hole in my throat and I can't read the keys on the cash register. "Mother of Christ," I say, pouring myself some soda. "Don't eat all those for my benefit. You'll have a bloody heart attack." But it's as if I'm talking in a foreign language again and this guy tucks into his meal like it's his last, which it may well be. I pick up a bar rag and wipe down the counter. Dumb sonofabitch, I think. No way this winner's going to be around for the second set. "Keep an eye on him," I tell the doorman. "He starts looking pale, you get him the hell out of here. Otherwise it's you cleaning up after him. You got that? Jesus."

The Green Bug

I got her answering machine and didn't feel like leaving a message. But I let the tape run its full thirty seconds before I hung up. Let her hear the sounds of a real dive and wonder who it is, I thought. I ordered an Absolut from the bartender and after that I talked to no one.

When the drink was gone I deposited another half-minute of bar noise on Helen's machine, then decided to go over to her place anyway. She didn't always answer the phone, I knew that. I suspected she used a secret ring, but she wouldn't tell me what it was.

I climbed on a bus headed for the north end. Three kids about sixteen in lumber jackets and black Doc Martens got on with me and headed straight for the back. When I looked in their direction one of them flashed open his jacket and I saw the silvery glint of a gun or a knife tucked into his pants. He grinned at me.

The last of the daylight had gathered grubbily in the square backyards of the wartime houses we passed once we cleared downtown. Ragged plum trees struggled to give some sense of the rural to what had, in the last twenty years, become little more than a ghetto. Dog shit was pushed into nasty little piles and thick weeds poked through the fences, that grey chainlink that defines property lines and makes a grim checkerboard of a neighbourhood.

Until I met Helen I had only driven through this part of the city, usually in a hurry to get somewhere on the other side. My wife Mary used to sell antiques in the market square on summer Sundays, and we had visited a few garage sales up here. But we quickly gave up any hope of finding anything we could actually use or sell. Old toasters and hair dryers were the usual dirty fare, piled on top of ashtrays stolen from motels along the St. Lawrence. Incomplete wrench sets leaving greasy stains on curtains riddled with cigarette burns.

But Helen loved it up here. She felt like a queen. She was pretty in a sophisticated, expensive way no one else this side of downtown ever managed, and she got frequent, nerve-wracking looks from men. She told me she had no doubt that given the wrong circumstances they would jump her and leave her "a changed woman," so she avoided the very darkest alleys, the sections of street with burned-out lights. But for the most part she wandered about her adopted kingdom freely and happily.

I asked her what the other women thought; *didn't they hate her?* She told me, "No, not really. Most of them just think I'm a spoiled university grad. They resent my money, if you can call two grand a month in support payments real money. But no, they don't hate me. I play bingo with them, for Christ's sake. I buy them drinks when I win. How could they hate me?"

When it became clear that I wouldn't be able to stop wanting her, I tried to find fault with her. I detested, for instance, the way she would cut her toenails and leave them in a little pile on her bedside table, sometimes for weeks. "But I'm usually alone," she explained when I called her on it. "It should make you happy." I asked her why those ragged crescent moons would ever make me happy, and she explained that they proved she was faithful to me. "If there were other men in my life I would clean up a bit more," she said.

And I hated how affectionate Helen was in public. When we walked the neighbourhood she threw her arms around me like a long scarf and covered my face with kisses. Occasionally she took my nose right into her mouth and sucked on it, leaving me both aroused and irritated.

One of the kids at the back of the bus licked some condensation from the windows. His friends laughed. He wrote TIHS on the glass with his tongue. I thought about pointing out that the S was the wrong way around, but when the three of them caught me studying them I quickly turned away.

Whenever we met downtown for a sneaked meal, a movie, Helen was more discreet, content to play an aggressive footsie under the table, to embarrass me with crude looks. There were other things: the way she played with her hair and the way she swore even more than I did; her refusal to read a newspaper. But none of them was enough to stop me from seeing her. It was just a way of keeping things in perspective. Helen would never be the woman of my dreams; Mary, though, just might be, given time. And I used these imperfections, the tiny cracks, to make myself feel comfortable with what I was doing. If Helen had been a little more special, or a lot less enticing — one or the other — none of this would have happened. No. Some of it would have happened, but it would have had a different ending.

Helen had her eye on me long before I noticed her. She revealed this the first day we slept together. She lay on her stomach, naked, and said she had watched me drinking with Mary at a night club we went to when I still liked to watch Mary dance. "I knew you guys were in trouble," she told me, "the way you were always so reluctant to answer her questions, as if it was a chore, something that kept you away from your real friends. And you only looked each other in the eye when one of you suggested going home; just to see if the other one was pissed off at something."

I asked her where the hell she was standing to get all this detail. And when she said sometimes she stood right beside me, even rubbed up against me, I couldn't believe I wouldn't have noticed something like that.

"So you hunted me?" I said, leaning over the red-flannel sheets to play with her hair, to move it away from her neck and look at the three tiny moles that hid there.

She laughed and looked over her shoulder at me. "You're so typical. It was a game, Allan, that's all."

"But what about on the boat?"

"What about it?"

"You were after me then."

"Well…" She thought about it, pushing her head deep into the pillow. "Maybe then, yes."

The bus struggled up a long slope. I hadn't realized before that this part of the city looked down on the business district and on the big houses along the edge of the lake. The air was thinner up here, more rare. We crested the hill and the old bus lurched as the gear changed. I saw the driver checking his rearview mirror every few seconds, watching for someone to start ripping seats or writing in ink instead of spit.

The boat was a rusting cruise ship that took three-hour jaunts around the Thousand Islands. It was usually full of camera-toting tourists, but in the evenings you couldn't see anything, so a local band was hired and everyone drank like fish until the boat got back to the city.

That night we tried to dance, but the lounge was so full of smoke, and the ride so rough, that we soon fled to the deck, as far away from the music as we could get. There were still people everywhere — the boat was always overbooked — but the air was fresher. Helen placed herself just up the railing from us and, every time I looked over at Mary, there she was, her hair blowing out behind her, seemingly lost in thought. Pretty soon I was thinking of things to say just so I could look over Mary's shoulder. When Helen eventually walked away and headed below deck, I said I was off to the bathroom.

She was waiting for me at the bottom of the stairs and said, "I know you're with your partner." She spoke quickly and efficiently, the way I imagined a spy would. "Here, take this." She handed me a scrap of paper and I glanced at it. It said simply *Helen* and gave a phone number and an address. I looked at her and she said, "Call me. Or come by." And that was it. She disappeared into the women's bathroom and I didn't see her again that night.

When I got back to the deck Mary wanted to know what was

wrong with me. She said I was shaking and asked if I was okay. I made up a bullshit story about some guy giving me a hard time downstairs. It gave me an excuse to be on the lookout for him the rest of the night, and I'm pretty sure Mary bought it.

I called Helen a week later, after I had scouted the address and discovered that she lived in an apartment above a little Asian restaurant.

"Do you drive a green Volkswagen?" she asked as soon as I had identified myself. I told her I did. "Yeah," she said, "I thought I saw you. How many more drive-bys were there that I didn't catch?"

"Jesus Christ," I said, "do you sit in the window all day?" I was mortified and I almost hung up. Maybe I should have, but she invited me over and I said okay.

When I arrived she brought me a cup of tea and led me around, pointing out dismal artwork given to her by friends and a pet cat I should be careful not to step on. I sensed this was a ritual of hers, a well-practised routine, and I checked the carpet for tracks left by the men I suspected must have come before me. The apartment was full of the smells of spring rolls and sweet and sour soup, which rose through gaps in the floor into her kitchen. Even so, it wasn't long before we were in bed, my teacup still half full and cooling on a chair under the window, my pants and underwear in a sordid knot on the painted floorboards. I lay there afterwards (the memory of those red flannel sheets surrounding me like a sea of blood still ambushes me sometimes) and wondered what the hell had gotten into me — which was the wrong question to ask, I guess. That was when she rolled onto her stomach and told me how long she had waited for this moment.

It ruined the afternoon for me. It scared me, and I got out of there as soon as I could.

She called me a few days later, just as Mary and I were sitting down to dinner, and so I began my secret life as an adulterer, a prick, a bastard, a cocksucker. Those were the terms Mary used when she found out what I was up to. If she had known about the others — all the women I flirted with towards the end, sometimes even had drinks with, pushing those liaisons to the very brink of the carnal, then pulling back — she might well have killed me instead of simply kicking me out.

I got off the bus at the end of Helen's street. It was always a relief to get up and walk again. The locales framed by the bus windows always took on the quality of a film, a grim one-reeler projected by my conscience to tell me I didn't belong out here, and that I should be more generous in my life. The children who lined the route reinforced this by looking up at the bus, searching, I thought, for my face among the returning factory workers, the crossing guards and short order cooks. As the bus pulled away I stared at the three hoodlums in the back seats. They gave me the finger and I pointed mockingly at the mis-spelled and melting graffiti on the window.

I couldn't see any lights on in Helen's apartment, and I thought it would be better to warn her of my arrival anyway, so I went into the restaurant and called her for the third time. I had developed a fear, I realized, of showing up unannounced.

The restaurant manager recognized me and said I could use the phone at the front counter. "Save your quarter, my friend," he said. I leaned on the glass display case and stared down at three packs of chewing gum, a few Twix and Mars bars. The dinner crowd began to file in behind me. I wondered where people in this part of the city got their taste for Vietnamese food. I thought they probably came here for a different reason than the people who flocked to the ethnic restaurants downtown. For these people it was just a cheap meal of a different flavour, while in the city's core it was a fashion statement, something to talk about at work the next day, or to ponder over a microbrew after the meal. All of this flashed through my head in the brief moments of peace before Helen picked up the phone.

I said "Hi," wondering if she would know who it was, because most of the time it had been her who called me. Mary was often home when that happened and I would pretend it was someone from work looking for a file. When I was laid off I pretended it was a prospective employer, and the next day I would get dressed up and trot off to an "interview". If Mary wondered why these business people called outside of business hours, or why they prompted me to talk so quietly, she never said so.

There was a long pause before Helen answered me.

"Allan?"

"Yes, it's Allan," I said. I waited. "How are you?"

"I'm okay. How are you?"

"Okay too."

"Where are you?"

"I'm downstairs."

"You're where?"

"Downstairs. In the restaurant." There was another pause. "You don't sound too pleased about that," I said.

"Was it you that called earlier?"

"A couple of times, yeah."

"What do you want?"

"Well, I wanted to talk to you," I said. "If that's all right." I tried to make it sound cheerful, like a bad joke she should forgive me for telling.

The restaurant manager gave me a look as he wandered by with a plate of something red and steaming. He raised his eyes to the heavens and I wasn't sure whether he was asking if I was talking to Helen upstairs, or if he was just expressing a general sympathy for me, an *I know what it's like to have to talk to a difficult person on the phone* expression. I ignored him, then looked at the ceiling myself. I tried to find the spot where Helen would be talking. Her couch, a ratty velvet creation, was against the wall upstairs, about where the lobster tank was in the restaurant's dining room. One night, the two of us had mapped out the whole apartment this way. Her television was over the cash register, her spider plant over the first table you came to in the dining room proper. Her bathroom was right above the restaurant's toilets, which made sense, and her shower rained onto the cloakroom ceiling. One night while we were fooling around on her couch, Helen joked that if we were too energetic we would go crashing right through the floor into the lobsters. "And in your state of tumescence, and the lobsters' panic, who knows what they might do," she said. I remember I told her she wasn't exactly invulnerable herself and tweaked at one of her nipples. She shrieked and we both burst into laughter. "Shhh," she said with mock seriousness and a finger in front of her mouth, "they'll hear us." I told her it was okay, we could pretend it was dinner theatre and sell tickets, have the manager hire an usher and guide patrons up after their meal. She thought that was hilarious.

"When?" said Helen. "You want to come up now?"

"Well, I did try and call first."

"And I did give the impression I wasn't here."

"Or you weren't answering the phone."

"Either way," she said, "it must have been pretty obvious I wasn't here to see anyone."

"No it wasn't," I told her. "Actually, I thought you might appreciate me calling you."

"Appreciate! Allan, for Christ's sake!" Helen shifted into another gear without warning. "Don't you remember? Your wife walked in on us. She saw me naked!" She paused, but began again before I thought of anything appropriate to say. "Do you have any idea how that made me feel? Do you? Shit! I've barely left the house since then. And I haven't been downtown at all. It makes me want to take showers with my clothes on. I'm not the same woman I was then, Allan. I'm sorry, but we went too far that day. And Mary! The poor woman! I can only imagine..."

I caught sight of myself in the mirror behind the cash register. "What about me? You think this is easy for me?"

"It's not the same. You caused it all to happen."

"What?" I stared angrily into space and had to remind myself to keep it quiet. A girl about three or four put down her menu and watched me. Her mother leaned over and whispered something in her ear that made her look away.

Helen's voice rattled around like an insect caught in the phone. "You said she wouldn't come home. Do you remember? I specifically asked you if she might come back and you said *No, there is no chance of that*. Do you remember telling me that, Allan? If you had said *I don't know*, or, *Yes, there's an incredibly slim chance she might walk in on us*, I would never have agreed to do it."

"You would never have agreed?" I laughed. "Christ! It was you who was so eager."

"Only because you said there was no risk. And anyway..." She thought for a second. "Oh, to hell with it! Do you hear this, Allan?"

After a moment's silence there was an almighty crash from upstairs, somewhere just in front of the aquarium.

"There! Did you hear that? That was the picture you gave me on my birthday." she yelled. "The one of you, remember? You remember what you said when you gave me that picture? Do you?" She was hysterical now. I could hear her real voice upstairs, a distant muddy accompaniment to the small, tinny noises coming from the receiver. "You said that it would prove you weren't ashamed to be seen with me, to make your presence known. All you really meant, of course, is that you didn't mind hanging out in my apartment with a big goofy smile on your face."

She laughed into the phone. "Well, there won't be any more hanging out here."

I'd stopped trying to speak. I concentrated on matching the things she was saying to the bumps everyone in the restaurant could hear. It sounded now as if she was jumping up and down.

"Watch out for the glass," I said, genuinely concerned. "You'll hurt yourself."

"Fuck you, Allan!" she screamed. I pressed the receiver to my ear as tightly as I could, hopeful no one in the restaurant would hear her. The manager was standing in the middle of the dining room shaking his head — he was her landlord, for God's sake — but he was decent enough not to look in my direction. Maybe he hadn't made the connection. The same little girl was pointing at something on her plate, and now her mother was looking at me. She was trying, no doubt, to see if I had anything to do with all the racket upstairs, watching my lips for obscenities. Other customers were smiling to themselves, sharing knowing looks with complete strangers.

"Helen," I began. But it was too late. She'd hung up. From above came the sound of something, maybe the phone, being hurled across the room into the far wall, the one occupied in the restaurant by a painting of a woman crossing a muddy river on the back of an elephant. At the far shore a group of ecstatic women waited for her, their hands in the air. A bedraggled man, slumped under the painting, jerked awake and looked around to see who was attacking him.

I tried Helen's number again. Busy. I looked in the mirror and saw how my hand gripped the receiver, the white knuckles like a small spine. When the manager approached I said, "One, please." He led me in silence to a table underneath Helen's kitchen sink and handed me a menu. "Enjoy your meal, sir."

I ordered a concoction of noodles and grilled pork. Great flecks of mint and crushed peanuts gave it the appearance of an exotic ice cream. It was what Helen ate whenever she came here with me. She didn't like the spicier dishes and when she discovered she could tolerate this one she stuck with it. It was a conservative gesture at odds with her public persona, and in a strange way I felt privileged. She never tried to prove she was a cosmopolitan diner, afraid of nothing. But maybe on the days I wasn't with her she ordered everything extra spicy.

I ate in silence, grunting at the waiter whenever he came by. And when I had finished eating I lingered, long after the restaurant had filled up and they could have used my table. I sat there with a heavy glass of vodka, spinning the liquid against the glass so long you might have watched for it to slow into crystal, to stiffen and finally set hard.

It was quieter upstairs and no one was paying any attention to me any more. I did hear the slam of the bathroom door and some minutes later the sound of Helen walking back across the apartment to the couch, but from then on it was just her stereo. If you didn't know someone lived up there, you probably wouldn't have been able to hear the music. But to me the bass was like a faint heartbeat, a way of knowing she was still alive.

I got up and walked to the front of the restaurant. I paid my bill and asked if I could make one more quick call: "To someone different this time," I said.

The manager smiled politely. He had to keep the line free at this time of night for people wanting to make reservations. "You understand," he said. I told him I did and walked out onto the dark street. Against a lamp-post across the street I thought I could make out the shape of the kid I'd seen on the bus, the one with the gun. This is more like it, I thought. This is how it's supposed to happen.

Africa

I'm the one driving but I look away from the road anyway. Amy has her head tipped back and is taking rapid, short breaths, trying to ward off a sneeze. "Just let it go," I tell her. "It's dangerous to hold it. Your eyes will pop out; you'll have an aneurysm." She flashes me a look before her whole body convulses and I feel the spray's thin diffused edges on the back of my right hand. Amy laughs and peers out from beneath her messed hair. She points at a few droplets on the windshield.

"That was wild," she says. "Did I get you?"

I lie and shake my head. "It's a good thing it's a new windshield. The old one might have shattered." She buries her face in a Kleenex and I wipe my hand on the side of the seat. "A hundred and sixty miles an hour," I say scientifically. "No getting out of the way of that baby."

We turn off the 401 just before Peterborough and rattle north. Amy is still sniffing and I ask if she's getting a cold.

"Allergies," she says. "I'll be okay once we get there."

It occurs to me I suspect sadness, even tears, in almost everything Amy does lately. I think she cries when I'm not around. She wants us to get married and says she has to have children before she turns thirty, which doesn't give us much time.

I look over again, convince myself it really is allergies. "Is your dad gonna be there?" I say, as we drive through one of a hundred hamlets that cling to this road the way lice cling to a strand of hair. He's a pathologist in Oshawa, on call most weekends and stuck in the city. The cottage we're headed for is the reason he's worked so hard, and now he's too busy to get there.

"I don't know. I think so," Amy says.

"Good."

Amy smiles, but her red nose makes me feel as if I'm driving her to a circus, like she's a clown, or a seal that's been practising too much with the beach ball.

When we bounce down the muddy private road to the lake I feel a knot tighten in my stomach, a nervousness I hadn't expected. And as we round the last bend I see Amy's mum, Rebecca, heading up the driveway.

"Jesus," I say. "They get a telescope or something? How the hell did they know we were here?"

Amy just shrugs and gets another smile ready. She winds down her window and sticks an arm out, waves madly, as if we're returning from a world cruise or a honeymoon. I pull into the parking spot hacked out of the forest and turn off the engine. I hear water splashing against the new dock. No birdsong, though. Amy says all the food gets blown to the other end of the lake.

When I climb into the light I hear Rebecca panting up the slope. She bustles towards us, all shiny pants and laboured breath.

She's wearing a pile of make-up and I assume company is coming. Then I remember I've never seen her any other way; there is a different woman under all that Estee Lauder, that Chanel No. 5, someone even her children never see. I wonder idly, in the time it takes us to reach each other on the driveway, if anyone here would even recognize her *au naturel*.

Rebecca grabs Amy and tries to hug the life from her. When she approaches me I keep my duffel bag between us and just lean in for a peck on the cheek. Amy scowls.

"How's the car running, Martin?"

"Great. Thanks again." I try to remember if we're behind on

the loan payments. Amy's parents have a pile of money put away for her somewhere, but it suits them better to lend us a bit here and there; they have more control that way. It ticks me off.

"Where's Dad?" Amy says.

"He's in the cottage. We had some workmen in this week, fixing up the new fireplace. They left quite a mess. I don't know if they realize it gives all the trades a bad name."

"What sort of a mess?" I say.

"Oh, you know, Martin, dust everywhere, grit in my saucepans, a coat on the television. It's like living in a mine."

"Oh great," Amy says.

I follow them down the steep rocky path to the cottage, praying Amy won't turn into her mother. I realize that suggests a willingness to stick around for the long haul and it shocks me. I hoist the bag to my shoulder and hear the mickey of rye clanking against a belt buckle.

It looks the same as last time we were here: the "art wall" with its native prints, its family snapshots, its watercolours by neighbouring cottagers; the wall of windows looking out over the lake; the exposed granite floors where glaciers once ran; the wicker furniture and the sixteen years of *National Geographic* piled up close to the new fireplace.

Peter is going at the chimney with a wire brush, rubbing away all the extra cement he complains the stone mason left behind. I tell him to be careful he doesn't scratch the rocks, and he looks at me, trying to figure out whether I'm serious. He puts the brush down and holds up his hands to show me his black palms.

"I look like Al Jolson," he says, and soft-shoes over to the sink, humming a tune I don't recognize. "Give me a second here."

I watch him wash his hands, lathering up to his elbows, working the soap in for more than a minute. Then he scrubs at his fingernails with a tiny blue brush and I think he must have learned this routine at the hospital. I imagine rogue cells from his most recent autopsy twisting into the stainless steel bowl —

bone, blood, liver, brain. I turn away and stare out the window. The lake is being churned by the wind and a gasoline slick surrounds the dock. The impurity of the world hits me in a dizzying wave and I have to shake my head clear, think about something else. Peter turns the taps off and Rebecca hands him a dish towel.

"So, Martin, how's work?"

"Pretty good... you know." I look him square in the eye and hold his gaze for a second. "Same old routine."

He knows I'm a waiter because I want time to paint, but he insists on treating it as my career. He saves classified ads from the Oshawa paper for me, and tells me I'd be good at anything I put my mind to. So far this year he's tried to push me into social work, journalism and forest management. "You'd be a natural," he always says.

Rebecca is fussing around in the fridge, pulling lids off Tupperware and sniffing at the contents. Some of the stuff stays where it is, the rest she carts over to the dining table. Amy has disappeared. She does this whenever we come. I don't know whether she's acclimatizing herself somewhere, or just letting her parents use up some of their energy on me, dodging the first interview like a reclusive film star. I've asked her not to leave me alone with them — it makes me anxious — but she says I'm imagining things and asks me, *What are my parents going to do, eat you?*

"Amy, lunch," Rebecca yodels. The toilet flushes and then Amy comes out, empty-handed but looking like she's been reading a book.

The first thing I notice when we sit down is mould on the cheese. I kick at Amy under the table and nod at the green fluff attached like a limpet mine to the cheddar. Amy kicks back and mutters, "Just don't eat it."

Peter turns the plate to see what the commotion is about. He chops at the rotten corner but I decide that isn't good enough. I've read somewhere that once you can see this stuff you've got to throw the whole brick away. I'm wondering what to say, how to explain the chemistry to the doctor, when Peter picks up the button of mould and pops it in his mouth. He chews on it, or sucks, for a second or two, and then swallows. All three of us watch his Adam's apple rise and fall. In my mind's eye the muscles in his throat catch hold of the growth and slowly, like a snake, move it towards his stomach.

"Nothing to worry about," Peter says. "Just like blue cheese." I shake my head at him but he insists: "Lots of B vitamins."

"It's not the same mould as blue cheese," I tell him, feeling a bit presumptuous, but pretty sure of my facts.

"Sure it is."

"No, this stuff can kill you."

"Peter knows what he's doing," Rebecca says.

I shake my head at both of them. "I don't think you should be eating that. Really."

Peter laughs and grabs a couple of olives. He doesn't want to hear any more. He thinks I'm being prissy, that I'm failing some test of manhood. He'll connect this outburst to my reluctance to try out the water skis, slot it into the top ten list of reasons I shouldn't be with his daughter: No. 4 — *scared of his food.*

Amy reaches diplomatically for the cheddar and cuts a sliver from the opposite end. She nibbles at it but when we stop eating most is still on her plate — hidden under limp lettuce and half-drowned in olive brine. I tear off a piece of tough bread and play with it.

Rebecca pours some water into the bodum and the coffee grit floats around like black snow, coal dust. She returns to the fridge and sniffs at the milk.

There's a knock at the door and I jump. I look out the back window and see a Nissan Pathfinder up the driveway, pulled in behind our wagon. I wonder why Rebecca didn't hear it coming and glance at Amy to see if she's thinking the same thing. Amy gets up and starts collecting our plates, pushing all the leftovers into the garbage can. "Who is it?" she says.

Everyone ignores her and Rebecca swishes up to the door. Peter rinses his hands quickly, dries them on his pant legs.

"You'll like this guy, Martin," he says.

"Oh yeah, how come?"

"He's creative, a cameraman for the CBC."

"Maybe he can get me a job."

"Maybe," Peter nods, not missing a beat, "but he's abroad a lot. He's a loner. War-torn parts of the world are his thing. I'll ask him, though."

"What's he doing here?"

"Getting away from it all, I suppose. Visiting us."

Rebecca guides the two newcomers into the cottage the way an usher leads moviegoers to their seats. The man is tall, thin, leathery. Most of his hair has gone. Not much of a target for snipers, I think. He's carrying a grey suitcase, aluminum, and I assume his camera's in there. He carries it over to the couch and puts it down, gently, babying it. I know Peter has a case like this too, but his is full of surgical instruments liberated from the hospital. He says it's the first-aid kit, and sure enough there are Band Aids and gauze in there, some antiseptic, a local anesthetic. But there are also syringes, forceps, a couple of scalpels and some surgical silk. I saw it open one morning when we were at the house in Oshawa. Peter was in the shower and the case was open on the kitchen table. It scared me, and I asked Amy about it. She just shrugged and said her dad liked to be prepared, to feel useful. I guess he envisions some horrendous accident with a meat carver or the speedboat, and thinks he might be called on to perform some impromptu daredevil surgery. It would be a big thrill for him, I decide, to work on a warm body.

The cameraman shakes my hand and says his name is Gregg, Gregg Hansom. I tell him it sounds familiar, maybe I've seen it on a documentary or something. He likes this. "Not much fame behind the camera any more," he says. "The world's too small."

Rebecca cuts in: "Explain that, Gregg. Martin looks puzzled," and I glare at her. A memory rears up: Rebecca and I have gone to a charity fashion show that Amy is in. A friend of Amy's is with us too. At the end of the show they have a draw and

Rebecca wins a prize, but rather than go up and get it herself she sends Amy's shy friend, literally pushes her up out of the seat. And then, when the poor girl gets back to us, blushing frantically at the attention, Rebecca takes the crystal vase from her and puts it down in the aisle beside her chair. "Thank you, dear," she says, as if she was too infirm to do it herself.

Gregg stares into space for a second, composing his answer. "All the wars today are over-run with photographers," he begins. "Used to be it was hard to get to some parts of the world, to some of the battlefields, and the one or two who did brave it got recognized. Now we all fly in together, a whole pool of us — CNN, Reuters, NBC, CBS, CBC. More of us than soldiers sometimes. We're just conduits for the information now, cogs; or at least that's how we're perceived. Dime a dozen."

"Dad has told me about you, though," Amy says. "He says you love your job."

"I do. Best thing in the world." He smiles at his wife and she puts her arm around his waist. Behind them, a car racing along the far shore appears to move from her head into Gregg's. "Kim works with me too," Peter says. "That helps."

I move in and shake Kim's hand. It turns out she writes for television, mostly news copy, and she produces bits for *The Fifth Estate*. She is almost as tall as Gregg, and perhaps older, fifty or so, but quite striking. Together they exude an energy the rest of us seem to lack. They seem so connected to each other and the world, so in control of the room. I want to walk away and hide. Join a monastery, enrol with Dale Carnegie and come back when I'm better at this.

"What do you do, Martin?" Kim asks.

"He's a waiter and a painter," Peter says.

I frown. "I'm a painter who waits."

"For your big break," Gregg says helpfully.

"Exactly."

"Oh, so is there some of your work on the wall here?" Kim points at the art wall, takes a step or two in that direction.

"No," Rebecca says hastily. "We wouldn't dream of crowding Martin in with all those other artists." She moves between Kim and the three stairs up to the paintings. "That stuff is just country art, you know? Stuff we've collected up here. Not serious art like Martin's."

"They don't have any of Martin's work," Amy says. "It's not their style. Right, Mum?"

I sense a fight in the offing and tell Kim that my stuff is pretty abstract, not for everyone. And that it doesn't offend me when it's not liked. She says I should send her photos of my work and Gregg promptly fishes a business card out of his wallet.

The phone rings. "It's like Union Station here today," Rebecca says, and I wonder if she wants everyone to feel guilty. It's the hospital, and two minutes later Peter's apologizing.

"A kid was killed in Toronto. I'm really sorry. When they put me on call I forgot you were coming up. I should be back after dinner."

He excuses himself, but there is an excitement about him now, a fever. He emerges from the bedroom wearing a clean pair of pants and then he shaves. He doesn't bother to shut the bathroom door and checks his hair in the mirror, whistling. This is a man about to cut open a dead boy, fish through the abdomen for a murder weapon, and he's acting like a schoolboy with a hot date.

The rest of us mill around not saying much. Gregg says he'll have to move the Nissan before Peter can leave and we all trudge outside. When Peter toots his horn and disappears into the trees I look around and note that Rebecca has tiptoed away. Her vanishing act is calculated. We are supposed to wonder now if everything is okay; to focus our attention on finding her. Rebecca is a powerful woman, head of the school board, the cancer society, but she seems out of her element away from the city.

I tamp down the cynicism, bury it away for later, and smile as sweetly as I can at Amy. "Where's your mum?"

"I don't know. I guess she's doing the dishes. Why?"

"No reason."

Amy cocks her head to one side and looks at me carefully, a zookeeper with a poisonous toad, but she doesn't say anything.

Kim and Gregg go off to unpack, swinging their arms like toy soldiers as they march down the driveway. About half-way to the cottage Kim throws Gregg a hip check and they crumple in a heap, laughing.

Amy thinks she'd better talk to her mother. "No avoiding it, I suppose. I'm just collecting adrenaline out here." I rub her back, massage her shoulders, call her *Champ*, then I go nose around the dock on my own.

It's a while before everyone comes out again. Then they appear together, in an exuberant wave that leaves me feeling excluded. I can't help but think they've been talking up a storm without me. I feel ganged up on, and as they approach I back up a step, feel the water lap at my heels.

"We're going to the graveyard," Rebecca says cheerily. "It's old as the hills. Gregg thinks he might be able to use it."

"I'm just curious," Gregg says apologetically.

I nod with a fake enthusiasm and follow them up the hill. When I catch up to Amy I ask her if this is some sort of competition Rebecca is having with Peter.

"What do you mean?"

"Well, he goes off to his autopsy and so she takes us to the graveyard. Proof that she's as acquainted with death as he is. Comfortable with her mortality, you know?"

Amy tells me to fuck off. "You can stay down here with the fish if you're going to be a prick all weekend," she hisses, forging ahead and linking arms with Kim. Kim looks over her shoulder and gives me a friendly smile, but then I'm on my own at the back of the pack.

Rebecca asks Gregg why he has the camera up here. He tells her he was shooting in Toronto this morning. Rebecca nods but looks disappointed. She steps off the road and picks thistles, wildflowers from the ditch. The house in Oshawa is full of wreaths made with this stuff. Amy's father has confided that it drives him crazy. He says he feels like he's living in the middle of a bad craft market. Pretty soon Rebecca has an armful of weeds and I catch Gregg giving Kim an *oh-my-God* look. This is Rebecca's party, though, and we trail her along the lane like courtiers — the journalist and his journalist wife, the obedient daughter, and me.

The graveyard is small, surrounded on three sides by forest. The sun has already gone from its half acre. There are perhaps thirty graves, some twenty of them Campbells. Most of the stones are thick and weathered; they lean at every possible angle. It's a playground for geometry students.

Gregg asks some polite questions but I can tell he's bored. We all know there is nothing special here. All small villages in this part of the country have little corners like this. I ask Kim if she too was working in Toronto this morning.

"No, I flew in this morning," she says. "It was just luck Gregg was there."

"Where were you?"

"I was in Chile." She bends down and scrapes moss out of the engravings on the most deteriorated headstone.

"What were you doing there?"

"We're going to shoot a documentary on the wine industry. I was doing research. We'll be down there again before the end of the year."

"You and Gregg?"

She nods. Amy is watching me, her mother talking in her ear, buzzing around like a mosquito.

"This poor kid," Kim says, pointing at the grave. "He was eighteen. Can you imagine?"

I shrug. "I don't think it was that uncommon to die early back then. Harder on the parents because there's no one to help with all the work. That's the tragedy." I have no idea if what I'm saying makes sense. I feel like a high school teacher and try to change the subject. "Isn't it hard working with your husband all the time?"

"We have our own projects. Right, Gregg?"

"What's that?" Gregg walks our way and I realize I have just witnessed a call for help.

"We don't bore each other, do we?" Kim says to her husband.

"I didn't mean..."

Kim laughs and rubs my shoulder. Gregg points out a new plot by the entrance, now the way out. "Don't know how we missed that one."

Rebecca sees our interest and we all converge at the recently turned ground. There are fresh flowers, blue lilies rising above red roses like the ragged plumes of a heartbeat. I pick out the name — Roberts — and wonder aloud how he likes being among all these Campbells. No one bothers to answer me.

Rebecca starts on about brass rubbings. "I have one of a knight from a little church we went to in England. I wonder where it is."

"I don't think you'd have much luck with most of these stones," Gregg tells her. "Too worn away."

"Like ghosts," Amy says.

A car speeds by, and road dust floats like ectoplasm over the gate, descends on us and the flowers. Their brilliance is immediately dimmed. What was vivid, alive one minute, is muted, a watercolour rendition of itself, the next. I laugh at my sudden need to find symbolism in the world. Amy looks at me queerly, trying to decide whether I'm being disrespectful.

"That was Peter. I'm sure it was," Rebecca says, surprised. She stands on tiptoes, trying to see a little further down the lane. "We'd better get back."

As we file out of the graveyard Rebecca bends down behind us and breaks off one of the bright lilies. She tries to hide it in the middle of the sheaf she has collected but Amy sees her and exclaims, "Mum!" We all turn around.

"He won't miss it," she says sheepishly. When that excuse doesn't look like it's going to fly she adds, "I'll make a wreath. I'll dedicate it to him."

Amy says she can't believe what she just saw, but she clams

up until we're half-way back to the cottage. Then she stops.

"So what was his name?" She has her hands on her hips, head jutted forward like a bird's. Her neck seems incredibly long.

"Whose?" says Rebecca. She is blushing.

"The dead boy's. For the dedication. What was his name?"

Rebecca is flustered. She tries to push past her daughter, telling her not to be silly. Gregg and Kim stand off to one side looking pained.

"Come on," insists Amy. "What was it?"

"Didn't you say it was Roberts, Rebecca?" It is Kim. She has moved in to protect her friend. She takes Rebecca by the arm and guides her past Amy. "I'm sure that's what you said."

I realize this is a generational thing now. The afternoon is devolving into some bad Shakespeare, a half-assed King Lear. I watch for Rebecca to lose it completely, to start ripping off her clothes.

Amy shakes her head. "You shouldn't save her like that," she calls after Kim. "It was wrong what she did."

Gregg points to the curve in the road. "There's Peter."

We all shift our attention. Peter has changed back into his cottage grubbies — the ten-year-old chinos with their three-year-old grease stains from the outboard motor, the broken-down Sperrys, the lime green John Deere T-shirt. He waves at us, although we are probably close enough to hear him.

"Is everything okay?" Rebecca calls. She breaks away and skips, like an unpopular schoolgirl, towards her husband.

He explains that he felt bad leaving us. "I stopped and called another pathologist. He owes me."

"Oh," laughs Kim. "So you traded bodies."

Peter joins in her laughter. "When you put it that way, it does sound crude. But they're all the same. It's not like we can rip each other off."

"Like trading a murder victim for a car accident?" Kim is pleased with herself and beams, but Rebecca has a wary, wild-eyed look about her, as if we have crossed some terrible line.

Gregg clears his throat. "I think we've gone about as far down this road as we need to."

Peter nods, still smiling.

"Well, that's wonderful," Rebecca says. "Now we can all do something together." She stops and points dramatically over the lake. "Have we taken you out there, Martin?"

"Out where? The lake?"

She comes and stands behind me, then puts her head alongside mine. I smell her perfume and at one point our cheeks touch. She points again. "To Africa."

I look around, bewildered. Peter turns to Gregg and Kim. "Well, these two certainly haven't been."

"To Africa?" Kim says.

Amy shakes her head. "It's what my parents call it. There's a river on the far side of the lake. Lots of tall grass, strange trees. Mum says she expects exotic deer, gazelles and zebras to pop up when she's over there."

Rebecca nods. "We go at least once a year."

Amy says, "It really is neat in there. We should go."

"Have you been to Africa, the real Africa?" Peter asks. I shake my head. Gregg says he was in Rwanda for a few months with Kim. "We didn't see any gazelles."

"Well, we should go then," Rebecca says, clapping.

"Why, are we going to see gazelles?" I say.

"No, but now that Peter's back it's the perfect opportunity," Rebecca chirps. "You wouldn't want to embark on a trip like that without your husband."

"It's quite a haul," Amy says.

By the time we get back to the cottage Gregg and Kim have excused themselves. "I was in Chile last night. I don't think I can manage Africa before dinner," Kim says with believable weariness.

Rebecca tells Amy, "It's just the four of us then. We'll be back before dark. Your father will do a barbecue. Maybe you and Martin can get the boat ready."

"We can always go tomorrow," Peter offers.

Gregg says we should go on without them. "This is an R and

R weekend for us. Nothing too strenuous. If it's okay with you guys, we'd just as soon stay here."

"Sure." Peter looks out over the lake. Clouds are building over the headland and the water is being chopped up by the breeze. "Everyone else is set on going today?"

"Yes dear, we are," Rebecca tells him. "It'll be fun. Next year we might be too old."

"Mum!" Amy slaps at her mother's arm. "Just ignore her, Dad."

Amy and I haul the aluminum rowboat out from under the cottage.

"Not exactly the *African Queen*, is it?" I say. Amy sneezes and I tell her, "I thought you got rid of that." I feel irritable and would rather curl up somewhere down the shore and read a book.

Rebecca barges through the door with an armful of lifejackets. She's found one of those Tilley adventurer hats and it sits jauntily atop her hair. "She looks like one of the Pirates of Penzance," I whisper, and Amy giggles.

Peter follows her out, waving two pine oars in the air. "Can't forget these."

We struggle into the lifejackets, they smell of mothballs and algae, and Rebecca pushes us awkwardly away from shore. "You got a shoeful, Mum." Amy points at the wet white plimsoll dripping onto the metal. The noise is like rain on a tin roof and seems exotic to me. African, even.

Kim is standing in the picture window. She waves and pulls the heavy curtains closed as if across a stage.

"You see that, Peter?" says Rebecca. "Why would they close out all the light like that?"

"To sleep, probably," Peter says. "They're busy people."

"Or to screw," Amy offers.

Peter draws in his breath.

"Well, at least they're married," Rebecca huffs.

For the first five minutes, as we putter into deeper, greyer water, I oscillate between real excitement and a full-blown panic attack. The wind has picked up. When the shoreline is too far away for me to swim to safety, I force myself to breathe deeply a few times, self-medicate against hyperventilation. These people have no idea what they're doing, I realize, and I'd better get a grip.

The water smacks against the bottom of the boat like a hand, and the collision of freshwater wave against aluminum hull sends vibrations up into my body through my shoes. Peter opens the throttle but the extra speed sends us into the swell at the wrong angle and weed-green water plumes over us. We buck unevenly, a sick rodeo horse, towards the very centre of the lake.

"We'll have to take it easy," Peter says, stating the obvious. "We're not sheltered out here. Our place is in a bay."

I look over his shoulder and can't even make out the cottage any more. I think about Kim and Gregg back inside, the way they didn't want to come on this voyage and how easily they turned down the invitation. I wonder when Amy and I last did that. We're too accommodating, that's the problem. Amy claims it's because her mum is always so overbearing, a bully, and she doesn't want to be like her. That's why Gregg and Kim must have left such a good impression on me, I guess, because Rebecca was intimidated by them.

I peer into the spray at Amy's mum. She's sitting in the nose of the boat, her legs curled underneath her like a fat denim cushion. Her pirate hat has blown off and lies at her feet like a dead gull. There is water in her hair, splashing her face. She squints but is too stubborn to turn away from the weather. She's like a wooden mermaid carved on the prow of an old ship. Her bulk blocks my view of the distant river, and it registers that Peter is travelling half blind as well, navigating by the shoreline on either side of our destination.

Amy's gone quiet. She stares stoically forward, just like her mother, and I wonder if similar ideas float through their heads. I shift my weight in the boat and compare their profiles.

The sun disappears and the water changes colour, approximating the boat's hue, only a steelier, more substantial grey. Peter steers gamely towards Africa and I catch his eye. He smiles grimly and I know he's trying to decide who's to blame for our being out here.

"Have you travelled much, Martin?" he asks.

"I was in the Yukon once," I tell him.

"And how was that?"

"Great."

We fall silent again. For twenty minutes no one says anything.

Eventually the water levels again, the wind broken by new shoreline. The roar in my ears drops away. Peter's hair has been blown back and it looks like he just climbed off a roller coaster. He grins madly, as if he's decided it's okay to enjoy himself because nobody's died. I feel tension drifting away, carried in the boat's wake to deeper water. I catch Amy's eye and she smiles weakly. Not sure, I think, if I'm going to hold this against her. I reach out and touch her knee. It's as physical as we ever get with each other in her parents' presence, but it seems to be enough; she lets go of the oarlock and blood floods back into her knuckles.

Peter releases the throttle and we drift quietly at the mouth of the river. Rebecca swivels on her aluminum bench to face us. Her face is soaked. This is what she must look like fresh out of the shower, I think. This is how Amy will look in thirty years.

"Well, we made it," Rebecca says. "I wasn't sure for a while there."

Peter laughs, relieved, and Amy looks at him like she's only now realizing her parents were scared. I know that she'll either freak out or say something inappropriately sweet. It's her pattern when she's stressed. I wait.

"Shit," Amy says eventually. Her mother looks at her reproachfully but Peter just laughs some more. "Exactly," he says. "Shit."

Rebecca pulls open her lifejacket. "So what do you think, Martin? Is it what you imagined it would be like?"

"I can't say my imagination was too busy worrying about it.

Reality was heady enough there." I kick my feet through the water pooled in the bottom of the boat. "Know what I mean?"

"Not one for the open water, are you?" Rebecca gloats, putting on a brave, sarcastic face.

"Hey," I say, and I'm about to launch into a diatribe about how leaky boats in a hundred feet of water are no better than airplanes with one wing, when I catch Amy out of the corner of my eye. She looks frightened. Not just worried, but actually afraid of what I might say and where it might lead. "Let's just say this was a new experience for me."

Rebecca looks pleased with the admission and runs a hand slowly through her hair, fingers splayed to act as teeth; she pulls on some tangles. Peter guides us slowly upstream. A couple of minutes and the lake is just a memory.

"It is kind of the way I imagine Africa," I admit. "No sign of the wildlife, though."

Amy says, "It makes me think of Louisiana. The Bayou. I expect crocodiles more than tigers. Look at that." She waves a finger at yellow reeds all along the shore. Two or three red-breasted birds swing atop the long stems picking at seeds. "And there." She points into the shallows, at flat-topped red rocks resting under the surface like rusty tables. "Can't you just see it? Six feet of teeth and muscle waiting for us to tip over. One swipe of its tail and *whammo!*" She smacks at the surface of the water and a weak spray flitters a few feet. Rebecca wipes dramatically at drops that land on her but seems to sense how ridiculous it would be to complain.

The trees close to the water are mostly dead. Their roots have rotted and only a few bare limbs claw at the sky's leaden cumulous ceiling. A crow swoops, like a vulture, into the forest further back.

"It's more primitive than anything," I offer. "Like nothing we see anywhere else. That's why we label it exotic. If we can't categorize it — say, *this is like...* — then we get worried. It makes us uncomfortable." I nod at my own analysis. Playing it back in my head I decide it's not great, but it beats the hell out of anything I've heard anyone else say.

"Speaking of fear, when are you two getting married?" Rebecca says. She grins at me and Amy, turning her gaze between us but keeping her expression constant.

"Soon," Amy says.

"Have you set a date?" her father asks.

"Not yet."

"But it *is* going to happen," Rebecca snaps. "Sometime this century?"

I can't figure out whether it's meant as a question or an order. Everything I know about her says it's a question, that she'd never suggest it as a course of action, but the tone is strange, ambiguous.

Amy shrugs. "Hope so."

Peter regards me exactly as I would expect a father to. He has caught the disappointment in his daughter's voice. And he's suspicious. Instantly I'm thankful he hasn't walked in on one of her crying jags. The crimson birds take off and flit ahead of us, more tropical butterflies than orioles.

"Look out!" Rebecca stabs sharply into the water, suddenly shallow and yellow, at a sandbar that reaches into the stream like a jaundiced finger. Peter throws us into reverse but he's too late. We're beached. The nose of the boat rears up. Only a few inches — we've been going too slowly to climb far out of the water — but enough to tip Rebecca off her bench and into the warming puddle around our feet.

Peter looks at her sheepishly. "Whoops."

I laugh. The identity I feel with Peter saddens me. It strikes me that Gregg and Kim would both laugh if this happened to them, but with the rest of the world, with the four of us, there is always a victim.

Rebecca recovers and sits up again. Water trickles from her pants and she grimaces, aware that she'll be uncomfortable until we get home.

I grab one of the oars, reach past Rebecca, and heave us easily from the sand.

"Good job," Peter enthuses.

When we round the next corner it's as if we have entered a Club Med compound in the middle of the jungle. There are sprawling log and stucco homes, glass-fronted cottages, pine huts, sleek speedboats and boxy pontoons lined up on both sides of us.

"Oh my God," Amy shrieks. "When did all this happen?"

"In the last year, I guess," Peter says. "The road must have been extended."

"It's disgusting. It's not wild any more."

Peter nods. "It's not the same, you're right. But someone probably felt that way about our place."

"But I thought we were the first ones to build on the lake," Amy whines.

"That doesn't make it right," I interject. "If a tree falls in the forest..."

Amy looks at me like I'm an idiot.

"Hey, you could make the argument that you started all this," I explain. "If your family hadn't bought your lot, then maybe nobody else would have either, and the lake would have been saved."

"If no one gets to see the lake then I don't think saving it does anybody much good, Martin," Rebecca says. "And anyway, everyone up here is very concerned with the preservation of the environment. We're here because we care."

This sounds a little trite, like the slogan from a campaign poster, and I tell her as much, figuring I've got nothing left to lose.

She scowls. "Not all politicians are evil, Martin," she says with real venom. "There are good and bad ones. Just like there are good and bad waiters."

Amy makes a fleshy T with her hands. "Okay, okay. Time out, people."

There is a brief silence. I smell meat cooking somewhere, and an old Genesis song seeps faintly from a nearby radio. Up among the trees I catch sight of a young boy chasing a huge beach ball. Every time he gets close enough to grab at the ball he knocks it away again with a knee, an uncoordinated foot.

"Mum, you look cold. Maybe we should head back. There can't be much daylight left."

"Loads," says Peter. "We're in another time zone here." If it's meant as a joke it falls flat, and dilutes to nothing in the air.

"Yes Peter," Rebecca says. "Perhaps your daughter's right. Can we?"

"Home, James," Peter says, still trying. He steers us towards the shore until long grass fringes into the boat, then he backs up. He completes a perfect three-point turn and heads us back towards the lake.

There is nothing exotic about our location any more. The trees just seem ruined, the water simply muddy, the birds inanely familiar. A few small perch, sunfish, knife through the shadows. Rebecca shivers and Amy tells her to move back in the boat so she'll be out of the spray, but Rebecca shakes her head and assumes her mermaid pose.

The lake is rougher. As soon as we feed out from the river whitecaps roll at us like long, violent scars. The first one to hit sends a few pints of water into the boat.

"That's not good," I say. I do the math. A couple hundred waves like that, I figure, and we'll sink. At this pace that puts us smack in the middle of the lake. The sky is a steel roof over us now, and the sun won't break through again.

"Maybe we should hug the shore," Amy worries. "It'll take longer, but who cares?"

Another wave batters us and Rebecca gets a faceful. This is going to leave dents, I think. It'll look like we were rammed a few times.

"You should swap places with Amy," Peter suggests to his wife. "We can't have all the weight up there like that."

Rebecca squints at him but she doesn't move.

Peter shoves at Amy's knee. "Swap with your mother."

"Peter," Rebecca says, her voice cracking, "if we start shifting our weight around we're liable to tip the damn boat. I'll put up with the spray."

"It's not the spray I'm worried about," Peter says. There is an urgency in his voice, the same tone he had when the call came from the hospital.

"Maybe Amy's right," I say. "We should stick close to the shoreline. At least then, if something happens..."

"Nothing's going to happen," Amy says, trying to convince herself. She looks pleadingly at her father. "Please, Dad."

Peter stares off into space and I feel the first drops of rain hit me. In a few seconds it's a stinging downpour, as if we've drifted under a waterfall.

Peter nods. "Okay." He turns us towards the shore and a wave washes over the side of the boat. The water's at least four or five inches deep now. When I put my feet flat on the bottom it creeps over my ankles. "Jesus," Peter says. The boat is rocking dangerously and another wave hits. I drop into the centre of the boat and grab each side, try to balance the weight. Amy looks panicky and I don't know what she's going to do. It worries me how little I know about her, how so much is based on watching her mother, who sits obstinately still, wooden, and probably won't move even if it means drowning us all.

"We're not going to make it that way," Peter shouts, pointing to the shore. "I don't think we have a choice. It's right through the middle or nothing."

The fact that he has to raise his voice sends my pulse soaring. *It's a fucking storm*, I think. *We're all going to drown*. It occurs to me I should jump overboard. It can't be more than a hundred yards back to the river, its banks, and that's the way the wind is blowing. To hell with them all.

"What about turning around?" Rebecca yells. "Go back up the river."

"We're not going back," Peter says matter-of-factly. "Martin, you'll have to bail out some of this water. Use your shoes." He points at his wife. "And then you two are going to switch positions. Okay, Amy?"

Amy nods. She looks like a dog dragged out on the lake for the first time, rabid and unpredictable. I know in that moment, and my heart begins to sink, that we are drifting away from each other: Amy and me. Amy, I'm sure, has no idea it's happening. But something in me has clicked, a valve has snapped shut and rusted at light-speed; I'll never look at her in quite the same way. Never again. So much for unconditional love. I try desperately to figure out what just happened. It has something to do with repulsion, I can get that far. We are like magnets, our poles somehow reversed by the storm.

Rebecca starts to mutter, something vain about how her weight shouldn't be an issue here.

"SHUT UP," Peter barks. "JUST SHUT THE HELL UP!"

I tug off a running shoe and start bailing. The grey-white laces whip repeatedly at my wrist. "I may as well be using a teacup," I shout.

"We don't have any," Peter yells back. "So make do."

The rain is coming down at an angle now, slanting at us like crystal blades, and I feel winded. But Peter gets us pointed towards the middle of the lake again, which, illogically, feels like an improvement.

Rebecca turns her back to us and I assume she is crying; I hate the fact that the rain will disguise her tears. Amy pulls at my other shoe and starts ladling water overboard. The wind roars at us. The lake is black.

Twenty minutes, though, and it becomes obvious we're not going to die. We're half-way, or close to it, and the water level in the bottom of the boat is pretty constant. Unless someone gets up to dance a jig we won't capsize. And Rebecca, surprisingly, is in the middle with me now. She and Amy crawled around each other like crabs, their backsides never leaving the aluminum. Their feet and hands splash in the shallows. Amy is at the bow with her knees tucked up under her chin, shivering. Rebecca has fallen against me like a rag doll, staring vacantly over her husband's shoulder. I get a whiff of her shampoo and the shower idea hits me again and I'm nauseated, seasick, just when I should be used to the constant lurching. How far she's fallen, I think. How she must long for the city. I pity her because she's become the weakest of us. Peter stood up to her and the tough façade crumbled. A bully, a fifty-five year-old bully. Amy's mother, her blueprint.

"Look." Rebecca waves a dripping hand at the shoreline, still a quarter mile off. The rain gusts past, and through those wet curtains I make out the unpaved road that has been carved into the forest to allow for the new cottages along the river.

"What is it?" Peter demands. He's still angry, which is surprising. It seems to me he has no choice but to forgive his wife, whatever failing he has detected; the fury should have blown over by now.

"It's Kim and Gregg," Rebecca says, astonishment changing the pitch of her voice.

"What?" Amy whips her head around and peers at the horizon. A blue car appears and then vanishes behind fresh rain, granite cliff, trees. It climbs and winds, becomes invisible and then visible again.

"I don't think so," Peter says, more calmly. "Nice idea, but that's not them."

And once he has said it, it becomes obvious. The car is too bright to be the Pathfinder. It's a station wagon, an old one.

"They couldn't do anything for us anyway," I say. "We're almost back."

"Good," Rebecca says. "Because I need a big goddamn whisky."

I laugh and agree with her.

"We don't have any whiskey," Peter tells her.

"I brought some," I say. "A small bottle. Crown Royal."

"Well that may not be enough — and it's not my brand — but good for you, Martin." Rebecca rubs me on the back and more cold water moves through to my shoulders.

Amy is looking at me, wondering why I brought booze up here, why I didn't tell her. I sense the cogs turning, ugly conclusions falling irreversibly into place. Sweat and rain mingle on my body. I am hot and cold at the same time, committed and resigned.

"Why did you bring it?" she says.

"In case of trauma," I tell her, joking. "Just call me Kreskin."

Rebecca laughs, almost giddy now. The dock is visible in the distance: the finishing line.

"But this isn't the sort of trauma you had in mind, is it?" Amy says.

I realize this is the attack I've been waiting for all afternoon. The rain — quite cruelly, it seems to me — has slowed to a mist, the water is a shimmering grey sheet, a square mile of tinfoil.

"No," I say simply. "It isn't."

Amy and I put our heads down and Peter guides us towards the cottage. I can hear the motor again. He turns the boat abruptly to the left and towards the shore. Our wake carries straight on without us, rippling eventually into nothing. Kim is in the picture window again, or still, hands on her hips, hair wild about her head.

"Perhaps our guests dreamed all this," Peter says ridiculously. "Wait till we tell them it really happened."

I ponder briefly whether people like Gregg and Kim could have this sort of dream. Behind the glass Kim waves enthusiastically and calls something over her shoulder. I wonder if it's something good. Gregg appears in the doorway. A couple of seconds and the smell of a fire reaches us.

Rebecca says something I don't catch. She stands suddenly upright and throws off her lifejacket; its scent wafts over me. She dives overboard, the boat rocking, and I watch her course under the surface, her red sweater fading, her twin white feet. Oxygen trails her like stars. When she arcs back to the surface, breaks the silvery skin, she makes almost no noise and her breathing is controlled, calm.

Amy shrieks — a little eruption, it seems, of pleasure, even pride — and then she too rises and tips head over heels into the lake. It makes no sense to me, this last-gasp solidarity. I'm stunned, my head thick with incomprehension. But before she surfaces and gulps ravenously at the air I am convinced she was more intent on leaving the boat than on emulating Rebecca. She is less graceful than her mother. Her dive's white crescent is flatter, louder, but the joy in her blood seems the same. The two of them swim alongside each other like dolphins, sister fish. Peter and I stare, first at each other, blankly, not wanting to ask the hard questions, then at the women's backs, the pumping legs. It always comes to this, I think. Two tired men in a tin boat. Two men watching two women swim away, joyously.

Monkey Boy

I'm eating lunch at The Asian, deciding it's not that bad, this quiet life, when Newman swishes past with Marie Thomas. I think that's her name. Sweet girl. She was at university with my brother, Tom. They dated for a few months, travelled together through Asia. Tom ended up marrying Sarah, a commerce student from Montreal, but now and again I catch him staring wistfully into space and I know he's thinking about Marie. Anyway, I see Newman with her and my good mood is gone. Just like that. I've lost my appetite.

The thing is, Newman fucks women around. Plain and simple. I remember how, not long after he came to town fresh from two years teaching English in Europe somewhere, he convinced everyone that he'd been wronged by the ex-husband of a social worker he'd dated three or four times. We're all giving this guy the evil eye, generally making the poor sap feel unwelcome, when the truth comes out. Newman was shoving the social worker around. One day the ex brings the kids back after having them for the weekend. He catches Newman flogging his wife with a tea towel. He's got her backed against the refrigerator, cowering like a dog. The ex throws Newman out and Newman charges him with assault. Boy, that prick can tell a story. I don't recall why the woman didn't clear that mess up before it got too nasty. Scared probably.

Another time, Newman's dating this waitress from a country and western bar. Naomi. And he convinces her that he's got cancer and he's going to die. No shit. Says he's got six months before his bones crumble and they put him in a wheelchair. Three months after that he's gonna be dead. Naomi's heartbroken. She gives him loads of money to get to Ottawa once a month for this special treatment he needs, as well as twenty bucks here and there for dope to dull the pain. As soon as I found out I told him to come clean. He says, *Okay*, and makes like he's confessed. Sure enough, they break up and I think, *Good for her*. Turns out he's fed her a line about not wanting to break her heart later, so it's better for them to separate now.

So, of course, when I see him with Marie all this shit comes flooding back. I get home and call Tom.

"Yeah, I remember that guy," he says. "Nasty piece of work." But all the same, he doesn't feel like there's much he can do. "If I get involved, Sarah will think I'm emotionally attached. You know what she's like."

"Well yeah, but what about Marie?" I ask. "You two were really close. Couldn't you call when Sarah's not around?"

"Then Newman's got me lying to my wife," Tom says.

And after that it doesn't matter what I tell him, or how many ways I point out that his logic is completely fucked: he says he can't get into it. "That's why I left that city," he says. "Too much bullshit."

I think about doing something myself. But it won't do me any good to call the guy; Newman and I had a final falling out months back. He tried to get April, my wife, to act as a reference for him on a job he wanted down at the customs office. Wanted her to say he used to work for her. Well, April's a vice-principal and her credibility is important. She was nice about it, but she said, "Sorry Newman, I won't lie for you." Then he starts calling her every name he can think of. Just lost it completely. I kicked him out and we stood yelling at each other on the street. Spit was flying everywhere. Haven't swapped a civil word since.

For some reason calling Marie never occurs to me. That would be the obvious solution. Maybe subconsciously I already want some more concrete revenge, something to balance the evil I figure Newman's responsible for. Who knows?

Without really thinking about it, I whip out the Olivetti and bang his name and address onto an envelope. I put two n's — Newmann — just to throw him off the scent. Inside, I drop one of the two fortunes I got today at The Asian. After all, they can't both be mine. I give Newman *The laws sometimes sleep but never die*, which sounds appropriately weird. I'd be a bit freaked out if I got that in the mail. I throw the other fortune in a teapot April never uses. *Your business will assume vast proportions* it says. And since I'm out of work I figure I can forget that one. If there's no entertainment value, I forget it. I'm not a super-stitious guy.

I spend the next three days wondering if Newman's got his fortune yet. I worry that he'll open the envelope and think it's empty. He'll try to interpret that absence of a letter, show the spelling mistake to a few people, and then forget all about it. I also wander the streets hoping to get another glimpse of Marie. I want to see her alone, or necking with a stranger in a bar. Anything like that. I look her up in the phone book and stroll past the address a few times, but no luck. I become a touch paranoid and give up that strategy. Last thing I want is some-one calling the cops. I mean, I can hear it already: *No sir, not prowling at all. I'm actually this girl's guardian angel; just looking out for her, sir.* Yeah, that'll go over big.

But it works, this sitting back and waiting. I'm in the restau-rant again, eating the same dish I always do, the number three. Four shrimp, celery, onions and strands of a dark bitter cabbage in a red curry sauce, piles of rice. $4.99! The place is always packed. And it's a one-man show. Pat does all the cooking in two jet-black woks, works his ass off. Last summer he returned to Cambodia to see family, closed the restaurant for six weeks in January and February. I swear a couple dozen locals were going through withdrawal.

Newman strides by while I'm fishing in my mouth for a shrimp tail. As *he* disappears Marie bounds past, a big giddy smile. She launches herself out of the frame and, I imagine vividly, into Newman's arms.

It's possible I'm jealous. When Marie was seeing Tom, my loyalty was to him — simple as that. It was black and white. The rest, I guess, I suppressed. Just now, though, something ugly lurched in my stomach. Knowing where her joy was directed, how misplaced it was.

Someone at the next table leaps up and presses the side of his face against the glass. He peers angrily down the street.

"That was him!" he says, obviously excited. He's a fiery-looking bastard: close-cropped red beard and boots that look like real snakeskin. "You see him?"

A pretty girl, yellow book open on her lap, looks up sleepily. "See who?"

"Newman! That's the guy I was telling you about."

"Oh. No, I didn't see him. Sorry."

"That guy is such an asshole." He opens the door and runs into the middle of the road so he can see all the way to the corner. "Fuck!" he screams. Even in here it's loud. Pat looks up from his wok.

When the guy has settled back down, I clear my throat. "You know Newman," I say, too damn curious, too stupid, to keep my mouth shut. The girl makes an excuse to leave, and me and Billy, that's his name, are soon swapping horror stories about Newman. The Naomi episode is hardest for him to swallow. She's the cowgirl waitress who thought Newman was dying. She's also this guy's sister. He's up from a town outside Chicago. Apparently he and Naomi were coming downtown on the bus one day this week and she pointed Newman out. Billy's already heard what Newman did to her. The bus driver didn't stop, said he didn't want a murder on his hands.

"You know where that cocksucker lives?" Billy asks, squinting over the table. "Naomi won't tell me, says she's *learnt* from him, that he made her stronger."

"How is Naomi?"

"Why?"

I shrug. "Just asking."

Billy tries to decide, I think, whether he can trust me. That's the sort of suspicion Newman prompts.

"Honest," I say.

He nods at his empty, red-stained plate. "Naomi's okay. Nothing keeps her down." I think about the way Billy ran out into the street. Those lizardy boots. Newman is in trouble, I know it.

"So. You know where he lives or not?"

"Yeah. But."

"But nothing, Monkey Boy. Give me the address."

I stare at him. "Monkey Boy? What the hell's Monkey Boy?"

He shrugs. "I dunno. Just seems to fit. It's like you want to swing about in the trees screeching, but you don't want to get involved. You're off somewhere chewing on a banana. Or yanking on it."

He laughs at his own joke, then he runs a finger nervously along his top lip.

"That's a lousy explanation," I tell him.

Billy opens his eyes wide, too wide, and stares outside. Not listening to me. Then he scrunches them closed and rubs at them with his knuckles. This guy's crazy, I think. But I give him the address anyway.

"Drive me over there," Billy says. "Come on." He pushes his chair noisily away from the table, slaps at my arm. "Chop-chop, Monkey Boy."

I look around, embarrassed. Already I blame Newman for getting me into this mess.

Billy has me park at the very end of the street.

"Stay here," he orders and wanders off. His bow-legged figure doesn't fit the suburbs. He reaches up and snaps a leaf from an overhanging branch. Spiked horse chestnut casings litter the road like tiny mines. A man at least eighty years old stops watering his lawn and watches Billy go by. Has to be checking out the boots, I decide. This isn't Norman Rockwell any more. I've seen films like this, and in them I'm supposed to be smoking, keeping the car running, trying to control the impulse I have to high-tail it out of here. Later Billy discovers me hiding in a warehouse by the water, crouched behind an oil drum marked with skull and crossbones. He kicks the can aside and starts in on me with a crowbar. When the job's done he heads back to his sister's bar and indulges a secret passion for line dancing. The cops come through the place, flash his picture, but everyone defends Billy, shields him. He was sticking up for his sister, after all. Who could blame a man for doing that?

I put the radio on, bring myself crashing back. The DJ is talking to a Saskatchewan pig farmer about methane gas emissions. Billy raps on the window. I didn't see him coming; he must have circled the whole crescent, gone onto Jackson and then snuck up behind me. I roll down the window.

"Well, he's in there," Billy says.

"How do you know?"

"I saw him. Doing the dishes. He's a messy bastard too. There were bubbles all over the floor, all over his shirt. Not built for the domestic sciences, our Newman. He live alone?"

I nod.

"Good." Billy drums on the roof of my car with his right hand; with his left he picks at a chili seed stuck between his teeth. He gets the seed on the tip of a finger and examines it in the sunlight. The yellow granule glistens in its bubble of spit.

"What are you going to do?" I say.

Billy sucks the seed from his finger and bites into its heat. I seem to feel the spice on my own tongue. "Gonna wait till it gets dark, Monkey Boy."

"Then?"

"Knock on his door, I guess. See if I can interest him in some fine encyclopedias."

"Books?"

"You bet. And I sure hope he buys from me, because I don't handle rejection as well as I should."

"But you don't really have books, do you?"

Billy bends enough at the waist to peer in at me like I'm an idiot. "Nope. Can't say I do."

"So, what if he's interested?" I say, feeling dim.

"Well, that would be his second mistake, wouldn't it?" He smacks the roof with an open palm and walks around to the passenger door, climbs in. "Want to grab a beer?"

I drive cautiously to the Bellamy's near the lake and we sit at the bar not talking. Billy heads to the bathroom and more than anything I want to smack myself in the head with the beer bottle. *If Newman wasn't such an asshole*, I think. And what's Billy got in mind exactly? He's just going to scare the guy, right? Shove him around a bit. Give him a shiner. Kind of funny, really, to think about Newman wandering around all bruised up for a few days. I'm not normally the vindictive type, but this is fate. Kismet. Too many things have come together, happened in a rush; it's like the elements are conspiring. If it got dark early now, if the sun were to dip, or the earth, whatever it takes, if the light failed, that would be the real sign. The situation requires violence. An eye for an eye, tooth for a tooth. Tom would tell me I was being an idiot. *Don't get involved*, he'd say. *Newman will trip up someday. There are people placed on earth to set these things right.* I've heard him talk this kind of shit. Like he thinks there are clergy mobsters out there, breaking legs in the name of the Lord.

Billy returns whistling "Blue Suede Shoes." "I'll be back in the States this time next week," he says cheerfully. How about you? Where are you going?"

"Going?"

"To hide up. You'll have to go somewhere."

"You're shitting me. Seriously. I don't know what it is you've got in mind, but Newman's not worth it."

"Tell that to Naomi."

"Sure," I say, leaving it at that, but wanting to add: *She's okay, though. She learnt, remember? She wouldn't want this.*

Billy builds up a head of steam. "And what about all the other poor bastards? Naomi told me this story about some kid he pushed off a balcony in the Alps, just because the kid stole his mail. You hear that one? Some junk mail didn't make it through Newman's letter slot. This kid comes along and tugs at it just as Newman opens his door. Tell me that kid deserves two broken arms, a busted spleen."

"You sure about that one?" I say, sceptically.

"Naomi's not going to shit me, if that's what you mean. She knows what I'm like. Hell, she doesn't want blood on her hands."

He holds his hands up. The nails are immaculate. This man grooms himself, I think. Or he gets it done professionally. That takes a certain type.

I swivel on my stool. "So what do you have planned here, Billy? Because I've got to tell you, I think maybe I gave you the wrong impression. I'm not cut out for this vengeance business. I might have thought I was. But I was wrong. I can admit that to you. Hey, I made a mistake."

Billy puffs out his chest. "We're going to put the fear of God in him, Monkey Boy. Scare him so bad he shits himself. Ever seen a man shit himself?"

"Umm..."

"Me neither, but I guarantee you, once a man does that he'll think twice before he pisses off a guy like me again."

"A guy like you?"

"A cowboy."

"You're a real cowboy, then? Cows and everything."

"Yessir." He reaches up where his hat should be, runs a thumb and forefinger along the imaginary brim.

Oh fuck, I think. Jesusshitfuckdamnchrist. This fucker's crazy. Cows! In Chicago!

"The light's going," he says. "We should get back there."

"I'm not going."

"Yes you are. Come on, Monkey Boy. Don't let fear get the

better of you. Think about who we're doing this for. All the innocents in your country. I get to go home soon, but you've got to live here. Come on, Monkey Boy, let's make it a better place." He grabs at my arm and I try to pull away. "Don't get obstinate on me, Boy. I can't do this alone."

He pulls me through the bar. In the parking lot he tells me to wait up, he needs smokes. "You run off on me and I'll be coming after you too. Naomi's counting on us now."

I watch him duck into Noor's Conveniences and I start the engine. Screw him, I think. I pull out of the parking spot, plan my route to the main road. But there he is, out already. He waves me over and I drive to the curb like a reluctant cab driver. He climbs in and throws a navy balaclava onto my lap.

"Matches mine," he says, laughing. "We're brothers now. Ain't nothing can stop us. But take the price tag off that thing."

He points through the windshield and all of a sudden he's doing a Patrick Stewart thing. "To Newman's place, warp 7," he orders, putting his hand back behind his head and then whipping it forwards. "Engage."

I look at him, scared but amused. I should just drive this idiot to the cop shop. Drop him off at the door. They'd know what to do with him.

He smacks at my leg. "Chop-chop, Monkey Boy. We ain't got all night now, you hear?"

He has me park in the same spot we used this afternoon. I figure my best bet is to tag along, make sure no one gets badly hurt. The bastard's not going to drop it, so I don't have a lot of choice. And I don't think I could go to the authorities even if he did release me. I mean, what would I say? How about: *I think this crazy cowboy from Chicago is going to kill a guy because he faked a terminal illness with his sister?* I don't think so. So I go along, assuming I can stop things if they go too far. Be the voice of reason. Now there's an irony: me going out of my way, risking life and limb, to protect Newman. I should've stayed in bed, that's what I should have done. *Idiot*, I scold myself. *Goddamned idiot.*

"What's that, Monks?" Billy says, and I glare at him. "Put on the mask," he says. "Then head up his driveway."

"In this car? In *my* car? No fucking way, Cowboy. You think I'm crazy?"

He waves his hands about. "Okay, okay." He pokes at the side of his skull. "Not thinking for a second. You're right. We'll walk. But bring the hat."

We follow the curve of the road. And, like a kid, I step repeatedly in Billy's lanky black shadow. "You realize you're going to have to do all the talking," I tell him.

"Why's that?"

"Newman knows my voice. And the way I move, too. So I should sort of fade into the background as much as possible here. I mean, I'm with you, but you do the talking and moving, okay?"

We put on our balaclavas and run like novice Navy Seals over Newman's lawn. In his boots Billy runs oddly, like his knees are about to give way. At the house he jumps up and down like a grasshopper, trying to get a look in the high front window.

"I don't see him."

"Knock on the door, then," I tell him, my hands shaking. "Encyclopedias, remember?"

"Right you are," Billy says, grinning, giving me thumbs up. "You're okay, Monkey Boy."

Newman answers immediately, as if he'd been waiting for us, and Billy pounces. A peregrine falcon dive-bombing a mouse, a lion ripping into an out-of-shape gazelle. The two of them crash into the wall of the hallway. I dart light-footed up the porch steps and into Newman's home, closing the door behind me. It smells like meat. Steak. The air is a little smoky, grey. I wonder if that'll piss Billy off. It's dumb, I know, but it goes through my head: what's Billy going to make of the dead cow smell?

Newman looks up, panicked; he doesn't recognize me. "What did I do? What did I do?" he whines.

"Ya fucked me sister," Billy intones, suddenly Scottish. "She didnay see ye coming, ya bastard." He slams a boot into Newman's gut. Newman folds into the foetal position. It's Billy's disguise, I realize, this Scottish thing. The dumb fuck wears his lizard boots in here — probably the only pair in the western world — and thinks a lousy Scottish brogue will keep him safe.

"Me an me partner," Billy says, "have had enough of ye bother, ya faggy git."

He kneels on Newman's shoulder and pounds a fist into Newman's temple. "Ain't that the case?" Billy nods at me. He winks through the twin navy slits of his balaclava. Green reptilian eyes. I see a pot boil over in the kitchen at the end of the hall; dirty foam hisses onto the element.

My mouth is too dry to speak much and, anyway, I'm still worried Newman will know me. "Aye," I croak, as Celtic as possible.

"So shut the fuck up and take yer porridge," Billy shouts.

His punches rain over Newman's head and shoulders.

"Stop!" Newman whimpers. "For God's sake stop."

He puts his hands over his head but Billy thumps him in the gut. The wind sputters out of him. Newman's bloody tongue flops over his bottom lip. From another room I hear music, cello suites. Billy sits astride Newman and pauses to catch his breath. A string of drool escapes his mouth and drips onto Newman's pale peach T-shirt.

"I just had surgery," Newman whimpers. "You had no way of knowing, but if I'm hit in the wrong place I'll be paralyzed for life."

Billy looks at me. "Ye hear that? The git says he's had surgery." He looks down at Newman. "You've had a rough life, son. What with the cancer scare and all." He puts a knee on either side of Newman's head, brackets it, then drops the heel of his fist on Newman's nose. When Newman tries to speak his mouth fills up with blood and he gags. Billy reaches for my hand, he slaps at it. "A spot of tag team," he says. "Some WWF to round out the afternoon."

I shake my head furiously, fall back against the door. "Noo," I say, trying desperately to stay in character. "Noo, I cannay." I sink towards the floor and get a sudden vivid image: a foul one-reeler of my grandfather hiking up his pant legs to watch wrestling on a Saturday afternoon. He used to get right into it, swearing and feinting, ducking flying clotheslines. Everything in front of me loses its unreality, the sense of theatre evaporates. And there I am, crouched on the ceramic tiles in Newman's front hall, my knees killing me. I'm intensely, painfully aware of myself. All the moral evolution of our family name comes down to me, to this gaudy, sordid moment. Primitive instincts that I should have evolved out of generations ago are going to ruin me.

I turn and push through the door, flail across the lawn. I collapse onto the hood of my car. When I look back I see the rectangle of yellow light flooding out of Newman's house. And in the bottom left corner of that geometry is Newman's bare right foot, limp, hanging over the doorstep.

I roll off the hood and scramble into the driver's seat. I feel awful. There's a spatter of blood on the front of my shirt. I start the car and drive slowly towards the house, leaving the headlights off. Billy emerges, lopes ape-like towards me, and smacks on the window. "Let me in ya bastard," he yells. "Let me the fuck in."

I drop him off at Naomi's house. I sit there with the car running while he tucks his shirt in. "This is between you and me, then," he says still breathing hard. "We're clear on that?"

I nod mutely.

"Good. On your guard, then, Monkey Boy. On your guard."

He gets out of the car and waves up at a high apartment window. That must be Naomi. I hide, move over a little in my seat so she won't get even a glimpse of me. Once again I pull away without the headlights on. Protect the licence plate, I think. That's the idea. A car heading the other way flashes its lights at me and I ignore it. When I finally do flick the lights on, the road comes up yellow, full of mayflies.

Four hours later I get a call from my brother. I take a look at the clock. "Tom! What's up?" It's almost one in the morning."

"Marie just called. Newman's in the hospital — in a bad way, too. You do something? She says two guys broke into his place and kicked the living shit out of him. You know anything about that?"

"Marie called you?"

"Yeah, Sarah's ticked."

"Why would Marie call you?"

"Beats me. Guess I left a lasting impression."

"It's been five years. You're in another city. What gives, Tom?"

Then it dawns on me. He got involved after all. I feel a flush of pride. "You called her, didn't you?" I chuckle. "Even though you said you wouldn't."

He pauses, then admits it. "Yep. And she said Newman's been getting strange phone calls, and last week someone sent him a threatening letter. He told Marie he had no idea what was going on. Of course, that's bullshit. I know that, you know that, but she doesn't know what to believe. She thinks the mob is after him. Or an ex-con. She's a sweet girl, little brother."

"Does she think maybe you're involved?" I ask. "I mean, one minute you're phoning to warn her about him — I assume that's what you did — and the next minute he's in hospital. Shit, you'll have the police knocking on *your* door in the morning."

Tom laughs. "Yeah. But when that happens I probably shouldn't tell them who or what prompted me to call her, right?"

"Hey, no one wants the cops banging on the door, Tom. But I've got nothing to hide." I squint at the dark television. "So where is he?"

"Hotel Dieu. Still in surgery. Apparently these bastards cracked his skull open. He's got spinal fluid coming out his nose. You imagine? I hear it tastes sweet. Like nectar, like the sugary stuff you put out for the hummingbirds."

"Lovely."

"Anyway, Marie's down there. Got her mum with her, but I

thought if you're not involved maybe you could lend a hand." I nod but remain quiet. "And by the by, little brother: you realize, I hope, that my beautiful wife isn't going to be inviting you for dinner anytime soon."

At the hospital I sit on a bench outside emergency, watch ambulances come and go. Through the window I can see Marie. She's reading *People* magazine and every few minutes she stares up at a TV suspended from the ceiling. I can tell she's really not concentrating, just going through the motions. Beside her is a woman I've never seen before, probably her mother. She has her arm around the back of Marie's chair. In the corner of the room are some kids' toys. A half-demolished red and yellow Lego castle and a few plastic palm trees.

I never thought about what this would do to Marie. That she could really care for Newman, might cry for him. Even so, this chaos is for the best. The truth will come out. Marie will realize that Newman had this coming. Hell, he was on his last legs anyway, what with all the chemo and surgery he told us about. We were putting him out of his misery. Like a diseased cat. The bottom line here is that he would have killed someone better than himself at some point. Newman's an asshole. It's high time a little light shone on that brain of his. If he makes it, great — he got his warning. But it's me I've got to worry about now. What this is going to do to me. You can't fantasize about a man's downfall for weeks on end if the real thing is going to land you in the psych ward.

Two-thirty in the morning I'm still there, still undiscovered. I can't bring myself to go in and comfort Marie. More than anything I want to touch her, wipe away tears, tell her I can make it all right if she'll trust me. Sit beside her and swap understanding smiles with her mother.

A yellow cab stops and a tall, frail-looking girl with a fresh cast on her left foot struggles from the back seat. She reaches back into the car and retrieves two wooden crutches and a vivid red beret. She places the cap on the taxi's roof and fumbles in her wallet for money, which she hands over. The driver nods, wheezes appreciatively, and pulls away. The girl yells after him and drops her crutches. The cabbie brakes, waits for her to hop alongside and snatch back her hat.

Then I recognize her. Jesus! It's Newman's sister. She must have come down from Ottawa. She looks terrible. I recall she has a disease that is slowly turning her bones to powder. She left town years ago, soon after being diagnosed; she said all the sympathy was killing her faster than the cancer. She's the inspiration, I bet, for some of Newman's more gruesome cons. His muse.

She hobbles into the waiting room. Be nice if Newman could last until she's gone, I think. From the look of her, she can't have long left. Marie spies her and jumps up from her chair. She squeals and runs, arms and legs akimbo. I'm convinced that she'll bowl over Newman's sister, knock her down with a grief-stricken lack of coordination. She's hysterical. The two of them grip each other and begin to bawl. A forgotten crutch leans against the window. Even from outside I can hear them. The wailing is muffled by the double-paned windows, but still it's sharp enough to penetrate me. *This is Newman's fault*, I say, holding back my own tears. He should be forced to watch this. They should wake that prick up and wheel him out of the oper-ating room, hold up his split melon head and say, *Look at this, you sorry bastard. Look what you did to these people. Do you see that? Do you?*

I get to my feet, wonder for an instant which way I should move. It always comes down to this decision: Which way do I go now? That's what we're all doing here, answering that one piddling little question over and over again. Which way now? Which way now? Red light? Green light? Red light, green light. Pathetic. Absolutely fucking pathetic. I stand there paralyzed, sunk in the smells of bleach and rainbowed gasoline. Well, I think to myself, you've come to the right place if you honestly can't move a muscle, Monkey Boy. I laugh cheerlessly into the night. The noise splinters, darts off along the black roads which head North and South. I hear it disappear.

Black is the Colour

I'm in the living room, thinking about how the walls could use a fresh coat of paint. And about infidelity. Mostly infidelity. Feet up on the couch, beer in hand, wondering if I have the nerve to fool around. It's not a really serious inquiry, just a time waster while Sam concocts some culinary masterpiece. I'm flicking through channels at the same time, ogling Mariah Carey's neon-lit midriff, getting a wicked crush on Wendy Mesley. It's all about women. I've noticed that lately. All my other hobbies are falling away. I haven't picked up the guitar in weeks, and even then it was to write a verse about a waitress at the Italian Pastry. I saw her again today, touched her small hand when she gave me change.

I'm wary about that stuff. For one thing, Sam's connected, she's got friends everywhere. Sometimes it feels like I'm dating a goodfella's daughter. I'm also a coward. If the coffee-toting girl ever returned the attention I lavish on her, I'd probably stammer a stream of inanities, blush madly, and then fumble clumsily for the door. I'd have to find somewhere else to hang out, start my life all over again.

I don't know what Sam's game is tonight, but I'm pretty sure she senses I'm distracted. Lately she keeps waving a hand in front of my face, going, "Earth to Spaceboy," or else tapping my head, saying, "Hellooo! Anyone home?" Annoys the shit out of me, that banging on the skull stuff. I mean, it's funny, but still. And when we're out, I can tell she's keeping closer tabs on me, checking out the things I look at, especially when it's other women. She used to just shake her head, write it off as a genetic failing, but it's different now. I'm wondering if she thinks I've stepped over some line. Or maybe she's seen something and misinterpreted it.

I can hear her banging around in the kitchen: the rubbery slap of the fridge door against its seal, the clatter of new black spatulas. Sam's been taking this cooking course. Goes out to a dilapidated farmhouse near the lake. From the outside the place looks awful, but apparently the kitchen is state of the art, all stainless steel and copper-bottom pots. Last week, though, she was thinking about giving it up. She complained it was a long way to go, and a lot of money too. "I want to spend more time with you," she said, tugging on the lapels of my jacket.

I told her, "You're crazy. You've been waiting all summer for this class to start." Right away she got this weird, suspicious look about her. I know she thought I was up to something. Getting paranoid on me. Not without reason, I suppose, given the way my brain's been acting up.

So I'm waiting, waiting, tapping my toes, sniffing for some hint of what's to come, wafting the air towards me with the sports section. And sure enough, Sam does finally appear, but it's pretty obvious she's already eaten. She wipes dramatically at her lips with a paper napkin, checks out the pink imprint. She sighs heavily. I shoot her a questioning look and head for the kitchen. There's a plate in the sink, knife and fork arranged politely on top. A smear of vivid sauce and a leafy sprig of parsley in the drain.

Damn, I think. Maybe I even say it out loud. "Damn." Not only did she eat, but look, she jazzed it up with garnishes. I spin-dry the parsley between two fingers, then lean over and sniff at the china. I run a finger across the plate. I taste tomato, basil, and something else I don't recognize.

"So what gives?" I ask, figuring there's no point playing games.

Sam blinks rapidly, like grit has blown into both eyes, but she doesn't answer. She purses her lips into a slim, uninviting horizon and pushes hard on the remote control. On the screen a pretty lab-coated woman is pointing with a shiny steel stick at a diagram of the human brain.

"Come on, what is it? I must have done something."

Sam regards me scornfully. She saw me chatting up the waitress, I decide. Must have. But I don't say anything, in case I've got it wrong. I'm no saint these days, and I'd probably land in even more trouble.

Sam hides behind the newspaper, but I doubt she's reading. I listen to the good-looking doctor prattle on about "the seat of deep emotion," stabbing at a purple, grape-sized section of brain. I fix on Sam's fingers, the scratched red nail polish.

"You going to tell me?"

I try to sound conciliatory, not confrontational. Something here doesn't seem right. All I did was flirt, for God's sake. It wasn't going anywhere. Sam's not to know that, but come on, we've been together long enough she should have guessed.

She slaps the paper noisily onto her lap, says, "I shouldn't have to tell you," and then disappears behind the headlines again.

"It's not your birthday, I know that."

I'm trying to be funny, to head off the storm. Sam stifles a fake laugh and throws the paper away. It folds in mid-air, collapses tent-like on the carpet. She springs from the chair and darts upstairs, slams the bathroom door. Her sudden athleticism surprises me. Lately I've noticed we seem to slouch around the house. And I've used the observation to rationalize my wandering eye. We're boring each other, the logic goes; we need to spice it up a bit. I wait ten minutes.

When it's obvious I'm not going to see her again, I lock up the house and turn off the television.

In our bedroom I come up with a scheme to relieve the tension. I don't know why I think this bit of idiocy will work — desperation, I guess. Anyway, I stick a stray golf club out the window and reach along the outside wall. Sure enough, it reaches the bathroom. I can see Sam in there, her slim grey shadow on the yellowing lace curtain. She's brushing her teeth, bending low over the sink to spit.

For a moment I sense that I'm making a big mistake, but I bury that instinct. I run the old Cobra six-iron over the glass, its metal heel like a monstrous fingernail. Sam doesn't hear anything. She's humming, the toothbrush in her mouth like a soft pink harmonica, going through some Nina Simone. She's just watched that film about the street urchin who's trained as a government assassin. The soundtrack was full of Simone's stuff. Yeah, that's exactly what she's doing, a bit from "Black is the Colour of My True Love's Hair." I listen, completely charmed. But when the music stops I rub the club over the glass again, punctuate that with a couple of sharp knocks. *Let me in* knocks. *I'm here for a cup of sugar, hope I'm not waking you* raps. For an instant there's absolute silence. Nothing. No tap water, no soft pumiced feet shuffling back and forth between the shower and the sink, no soft harp tunefulness. Only blood rushing in my ears, and adrenaline squirting into the 85 percent or whatever it is of my brain that atrophies while I watch *Wheel of Fortune*.

Then she screams. Loud. And what's really weird is that I hear the terrified yell twice. Once through the window, as if a stranger is being attacked outside, and once through the hallway that connects our bedroom to the bathroom. The scream of my girlfriend, the only person in the world I'm truly intimate with.

I go freezer cold, realize this mouse of a joke, this harmless prank, has gone terribly wrong. I dispose of the club, toss it into the empty slot of darkness behind the laundry hamper. The head twists menacingly above the wicker basket.

"Hey!" I yell, figuring to let Sam know I'm here if she needs me, her fearless protector. I lope over the carpet and along the hall, barge into the bathroom. I close the door behind me as if to contain the panic I've caused, set up a quarantine for it. I put an arm around her. Sam's hyperventilating, shoulders heaving. The toilet lid's down and she's using it like a chair.

"What is it?" I say. I feel like a bad poker player. Steve McQueen, I think. James Garner, Paul Newman. Hoping for something to rub off, using the names like worry stones.

"You bastard," she sobs.

"What?"

"That was you, wasn't it?" She turns her wet glistening face.

"What was me?"

"The knocking!" Her breath, a scorching mint, hits me head-on.

"Knocking?" I scurry blindly for an alibi. Perhaps tree limbs are being blown around out there in the laneway. I try to picture it in daylight. Or is there another window? Maybe I can blame a neighbour. It occurs to me that this is pretty much the fight we would have if I were ever unfaithful. The same angry tears, the pointed accusations. I'd make similar denials too, but Sam, knowing her, would pull some high resolution black and white proofs from her robe and wave them in my face. Which means adultery just isn't a viable option for me; I'd be lousy at it. But hey, that's great news, the best. I want to shake her by the shoulders, say, "Listen! I just realized I could never hurt you. Isn't that wonderful?"

Sam is oblivious to the epiphany. She spins the toilet roll and six, seven sheets unfurl like a banner, a snowy scarf. She tears them free and swabs at her eyes, blows her nose. Her foot is on the floor at that peculiar angle where it irritates a nerve and her knee bobs frantically. She slaps at my arm. "You're going to feed me a line, aren't you? Well, don't bother. I know what you did."

"Okay." I lower my head and own up to the prank, spilling the truth slowly, contritely, hoping to calm her with the delivery. "I didn't realize it would scare you like this. I'm sorry. I thought you'd laugh. I was trying to make it easier for us to talk."

"By terrorizing me!"

I shrug, struck suddenly dumb, but excited as well. There's so much to tell her. We can make plans for the future now. This is a great day. And she'll see that, after I've explained how this is a real turning point for me.

Sam glares, though, as if I'm a complete stranger. She rises slowly to her feet and stands in front of me. Twice more I feel the warm breeze of her exhalations on my face before she shoulders past. Seconds later I hear the chain on the front door. From the spare bedroom I see her marching towards Princess Street, arms like busy pendulums. She's half-way to the corner before I realize I'd better do something. I haul up the window as far as I can. It sticks two or three times, seems to conspire against me.

"Sam!" I shout through the narrow opening I've made. The wind carries my voice away from her, towards the lake. I try again, but absurdly I call out more quietly, so the neighbours won't gossip. "Samantha."

I step back into the gloom, register the sound of the shower dripping sadly into the bathtub. I've been promising to fix that leak for weeks, months even. Hell, if only it were all that simple. But it is, it is! I feel deep within me a tiny blue charge of discovery and resolve. I bound down to the living room, pull back the plush velvet curtain. I stare eagerly out at the empty damp street, wait for Sam to come back to me. I nod emphatically into the darkness. This is going to be so good. I just know it.

Going

He's a bullshitter, this kid two tables away. Funny how I can tell without hearing him, not even seeing him move. Something in the face. Certainly not the clothes, which wouldn't sell if it were that easy. Around the mouth, I feel. I'm like a microscope clicking onto a higher magnification. Or the downward swoop of lines around the eyes. Mischief. Worse. The whole street-facing room smells intensely of coffee and croissants. In the bathroom it's like chocolate.

Anyway, he's trying, brazenly, soft chin fluff and bravado, gum-snapping nerve, to impress a book-drunk girl. His T-shirt reads WITNESS PROTECTION PROGRAM, his baseball cap FBI. That boy, I think to myself, over the soiled brim of *The Globe*, just needs a big ol' tattoo. I watch, half bored. And then I scoot, before anyone can shoot out the stencilled windows (Roman *biscotti, cappuccino,* etched cumulo-nimbus of froth), sending see-through isosceles shards, whole geometry sets, whistling past, clattering clean into dense cooling java, gelatinous. As in *El Mariachi, Before the Rain*.

So I'm out, prowling the dog-wide snow-humped sidewalks, and I spy through the open chicken-wire door, green frame, of a Chinese laundry, two girls playing flute, some Schubert. Music muted by to-be-altered and frayed-hemmed suits, shiny and shabby men's workcloth. Houndstooth, broad pinstripe.

And kitty-corner, in an egg-drizzled phone booth, a man, fifties, green cords, mutton chops, moans *Oh God, Oh my dearsweetmotherofjesus God*. White-knuckling the Bakelite receiver. Is he hearing something, I wonder, about that brassy would-be gigolo of The Italian Pastry? Are the police stringing the streets festive with yellow ribbons down there, day sergeant megaphoning, *Game over, G-Man? You hear me? Finito?* Our city like an instant day-of-the-dead resort town, shops full of nightstick clowns, streets eroding through tar top to soil dense with trilobites and where we came from.

Yeti

You tell great stories of coming east in that white GMC van, you really do. Thundering through the Rockies like a motorized snowball. Stopping couple of times every day to let the dogs piss or shit. How one time Leda saw that horned goat scrambling across the scree and took off, forgot all her training and was gone three hours, returned with a red gash in her side from either the goat or granite. She was foaming, too, like she'd incubated rabies up there, and lay on her side panting while you and Kelli made love in the back, the foot-high curtains wide open so the gods could watch you rocking. Be like a sitcom for them, you said, a cheap diversion from the grand scheme, the big picture.

Was it in Dakota you got sidetracked, caught up in the Native Rights thing, spent a week smoking wicked dope and considering advocacy work? Meantime letting them use your van to haul whisky over the border.

And in New York City the 12-lane freeways made you so anxious a 52nd-floor doctor had to prescribe sedatives you still take when food freaks you out, or the thought of tomorrow. Took four of those pills just to get you back in the elevator, glass-sided thing like a monumental test tube, but strapped to that skyscraper like a knife to an armoured leg.

This is good stuff, nourishing I bet, when you're laid up for a while, summoning the nerve for next time. I got to hear it all, one night when we were half drunk on whisky bought with your first welfare cheque.

"Funny how it works so slowly when you feel guilty about buying it," you said, holding the smeared glass face-high, the world beyond slowly honeying. You played Bach and Lyle Lovett, Guided By Voices, kept me guessing tunes till Kelli went out, driven crazy by the volume.

"You should write this next story down," you advised, doubting, I suppose, all your own dusty equipment. "Use it. Really. Listen to this." You turned down the stereo to where it was soundtrack, nothing more. "A man and his girl are fighting. They're sitting in his pick-up truck, something *Lumber* written on the side. *Heavy Lumber*, maybe. It's dark, still cold. Frigid. He's got a beard and the frost catches in it, becomes solid, a dense web around his mouth. The windshield fogs over slowly, reducing them eventually to silhouettes, puppets. Just the occasional flash of colour, his red and black lumber jacket, her orange hair. But you know they're still going at it. He's trying to get the truck warmed up and as the argument boils he revs the engine violently, hides their voices under the automotive roar. His rage is connected through the muscle in his thigh to the noise, to the puffing white cloud behind. His brain sending out two signals at the same time. They become part of the machine. Metal dragon. Eventually she gets out and he drives away, fresh snow crunching under the tires."

You held out your hands. "Well?" Nodded some. "Great scene, isn't it? Sort it out, man, put it in a story for me."

I told you to have a go at it yourself. "You didn't come all this way to give everything away. Surely."

But you wanted nothing to do with it. "Just keep it alive," you grumbled. "Because that's the last time I'll tell it to anybody."

Yesterday we went for lunch. Outside the health food store a kid, all muscles, was unloading vegetables from your van. The brightest carrots I'd ever seen, radishes like swollen fists.

"Hey, it stayed in town," I said. "Who bought it in the end?"

You shook your head.

"Well it's doing good work," I offered weakly.

I was trying hard to be nice, aching all morning to understand a man gone empty inside, not caring any more about the world around him, divesting himself of everything. You stopped, though, on the sidewalk, and rubbed a minute at your forehead, really pushed on it. Then glared at me as if I was a total stranger who'd just fucked you over for no good reason. You took off down the street, limping. Out of the blue you're swinging one stiff leg wide, making people step aside. What the hell's that all about?

Pint

I'm in The Parrot with Jenny. It's about 6:30 on a Tuesday and a lot busier than we expected.

"So much for the quiet drink."

Jenny flashes me a look. Then she yells in the direction of the bartender, "What gives?"

The bitter-faced barman tugs at the bottom of his stained waistcoat. He points with his other hand at the TV set, hung high over everyone's heads on dull metal chains. "England and Italy," he says. "Football." When Jenny shrugs he adds, "World Cup Qualifying. It's a big deal for the regulars." He wipes down the bar between us, removes a piled-up ashtray, but strides away without waiting for an order.

"Which means we're not, I suppose," I whisper-shout in Jenny's ear.

"What?"

"Regulars," I yell. "I guess he's saying we're not regulars."

Jenny eyes me suspiciously. "You be careful you don't bore yourself to death one day," she says. "He gets enough of our money. The guy's just a jerk."

I try to remember his name but the noise of the crowd makes that sort of recollection difficult. Brad, Brendan, something like that. He has a girlfriend who works at The Tropics. Pretty woman too, but that doesn't stop him from wandering.

Jenny elbows right up to the bar, hikes a foot onto the brass rail that runs the whole mahogany length like a belt. Then she drags me in after her. She looks down towards the cash register. "Hey, a gin and tonic and a pint of the dark stuff," she says, knocking daintily on the Guinness tap. She pulls away for an instant, then leans in again. "Please," she says, and flashes that you-can't-hate-me-however-hard-you-try grin. It works, trust me. All sorts of bother has been avoided with that flash of teeth.

I check out the crowd; it's thinning. Game must be over. I ask the guy next to me who won, and he grumbles, without looking up from his glass, "They did." I nod solemnly, as if in commiseration, but there's no way he sees me or cares what I do. I note that all the tables are in use, but faces are just pale ovals in this light, ghosts in a carcinogenic blue fog.

"What're you looking for?" Jenny wants to know. I feel her breath hot on my face. "Not still worried are we?"

It takes me a minute to clue in. Then I scoff, "That? No, of course not." But I am, and I look about again, peer more seriously into the dark room. At the nearest table I take in a kid with a bloody, clownish smear of ketchup around his mouth and a mittful of french fries. Next to him, an old man with a runny nose and two teary eyes sits before a half pint of something rust-coloured. A tough-looking woman plays the pinball machine, jerks her hips at the game.

Jenny laughs brightly. "Bullshit," she says. "Look at you. Bundle of nerves."

"It's you he wants," I remind her, and that seems to tie things up for a few seconds.

"What's this, then?" the barman says, sticking his nose in. "Sounds interesting."

I assume Jenny will tell him to shove off, and I turn my stool for a better view. But I'm wrong and Jenny asks, "You got a couple of minutes?"

He nods and his name comes floating at me: Barry. It's as if getting a quarter pint of Guinness into me has opened memory's door. I begin to gnaw at the inside of my cheek. Jenny launches breezily into her story.

"I saw an ad in the paper," she says. "Six pitbull puppies, a two-foot South American alligator and an aquarium. All for sale at the same place. Can you imagine? This was on what, Saturday?" She looks to me for confirmation.

"Yeah, Saturday," I tell her.

"So I call the number. I'm like, *Hey, I want to buy all your stuff, but I'm a little worried the dogs will eat the reptile. Or vice versa.* The guy gives me this big song and dance about making sure I keep the alligator in the aquarium. *Otherwise you got a tragedy on your hands, lady,* he says."

Barry laughs, straightens his crimson wave-pattern tie. "Oh, that's good."

"It gets better," I tell him moodily.

Jenny giggles, takes a big swig of gin, full of herself. "Then I decide I'm going to have some real fun," she says. "I ask this pitbull guy: *You got some dope for us too? And maybe a Sony TV. And tell me, do you keep regular hours, or do I need to make an appointment? How about pizza, you make a good pizza?*"

Barry thinks this is one of the funniest stories he's ever heard. "The pitbull guy," he chuckles. "That's good."

"You should have seen her," I tell him, gesturing at Jenny with a cocked thumb, unable to stop myself. "She was flat on the living room floor kicking her legs in the air. Laughing her head off. She looked like a big prankster bug."

Barry wipes his forehead with the beery bar rag and right away I'm pretty sure he didn't mean to do that. He wags a finger at Jenny as he walks away. "You are an evil woman," he says.

"Well, now you've done it," I tell Jenny. "Why didn't you just rent a billboard over the highway?"

She pokes me in the chest with two fingers, so hard it feels like a rib cracked. "Because this was more fun."

I turn away. There's no changing what just happened. Jenny

says I'm a worrier and it's true. Every dog turd I see now is a sign this guy's closing in.

The light softens outside. On the patio a pretty woman in a navy suit frowns as she swats at late-summer wasps that fly drowsy, weaving missions at her head. Her boyfriend seems oblivious, even to the exaggerated head-jerk she makes when one of the yellowjackets dives for the gap between her sugary pink lips. She tries to compose herself repeatedly, to concentrate on her companion's distinct drone. It occurs to me that I already know her better than he does. Even through the double-paned window, despite the different worlds we occupy, I know what she wants and also that he hasn't a clue. "Take her away from here, man," I mutter. Jenny raises an eyebrow.

I want to ask Jenny, *Why don't I understand you? How is it I can stand beside you every day for months and still be baffled by your actions?* But Barry high-steps past and I keep quiet. I stare at Jenny's delicate hand as she swirls what's left of her gin. A lemon slice beached on diminishing soft-sided ice.

Someone new sidles up to the bar. He reeks of tequila. Salt has caked in his sadly extravagant moustache. "Hey," he says, and I nod curtly. He taps me on the arm. "Hey, I bin arrested seventeen times for defendin' women."

"Beautiful," I say.

Jenny looks over suspiciously, worried it's her presence that prompted this confession.

"Seventeen," he says again. "An' eleven times I was convicted. Can you believe it?"

I shake my head but he's not looking for feedback. "They sent me to see shrinks too. An' I reckon I must belong in another time, because they all told me I was a neanderthal." He puts his head on the bar and giggles like a boy.

Barry plunks down a tequila, looks around for the salt shaker. "How do, Lionel," he says, sporting a sudden English accent. "One of these, is it?"

"Are you crazy?" Jenny hisses. "Is he driving?"

"Cabbing."

"Even so."

I watch this exchange like it's a tennis match. But I watch Lionel too, wait for him to do something ugly. His head, though, remains attached to the bar.

Barry glares my way like I'm the unpredictable element here. I tell Jenny she should stay out of it. "It's his world," I say. But Jenny waves me off.

Barry puts an elbow down on the bar, rests his red cheek against a pale balled fist. "Funny thing about that story of yours," he says seriously.

"What's that?" I feel like I'm at the end of my rope. Like one wrong word is all it will take.

"I know the guy, that's what. He comes in here."

Jenny and I must look incredulous because Barry nods earnestly. "He does. Most days actually."

"Really," Jenny says, her face one big smirk.

"Sure. Matter of fact..." Barry peers down the length of the bar, then leans back to check out the dartboards, and the small stage where the bands set up. "He might even be here now."

I'm already half off my stool, tugging at Jenny's arm. Barry grins, pleased with himself.

"You having fun?" I growl.

"Yeah, somewhat," Barry admits. "Your predicament's not my doing, though, is it?"

"So you're lying."

"No, I'm not. Actually, Jack often brings a couple of his dogs down with him. Chains them up end of the patio."

"I bet that's good for business," Jenny says.

"We set up an area," Barry explains.

"Oh, I see. Like a smoking area, but for dogs," Jenny says, getting louder. "That sounds likely."

Barry stands up very straight. He gestures with his hands, shows us the palms, fingers pointed at the ground. It's meant to say, "Hey, I'm just the messenger here," but also has the effect of making him seem crippled somehow, as if he has no shoulders. The phone rings and he shuffles off to the corner.

A second later, he exclaims, "Jack! Wow! We were just talking about you."

Jenny snorts, slaps her drink down. Lionel moans beside me, twitches sharply, but keeps his eyes screwed shut. You're a smart man, I think.

Barry goes on, "You psychic or something, Jack? Your ears burning, are they? No, it was all good. Well, interesting anyway." He pauses to listen.

Jenny sucks vigorously on her straw, gets hold of a noisy mix of air and water. Her eyes are big as beer coasters.

"Did you put an ad in the newspaper, Jack? Yeah, that's the one."

"Let's get the hell out of here," I say.

"We can't," Jenny says. "Shut up."

Barry grins. He looks at us and points dramatically at the receiver. Suddenly the bar seems deserted, all extraneous sound sucked from the world. Anything I register now could be coming straight from Jack's living room. I force myself to breathe.

"She's here," says Barry. "Yeah, I know. Weird. Actually, there's two of them. Some guy."

"He's having us on," Jenny says.

Barry hears her. He winks at me. "Yeah, that's what I'm doing," he says. "I'm playing a game."

I feel dragged into a conspiracy I don't understand. One where I end up the patsy.

"Uh-huh," he says into the phone. "Uh-huh."

Jenny rolls her eyes like she's amazed anyone would try this lame a gag, but I think maybe she's reading it all wrong. Two middle-aged guys in baseball uniforms, with enormous twin guts, hold up empty glasses at the end of the bar. "Look at that," I say. "If Barry is toying with us, it's costing the joint money."

"Yeah, I suppose I can try," Barry says. He lifts his wrist, checks the time. "Fifteen minutes? Sure. No, you can't bring them in here. Yeah, I understand, but still. Good. Thanks. I appreciate that. Yeah, okay. See you, Jack." He hangs up.

I feel the future splinter as we sit there. That was or wasn't Jack. He is or isn't on his way here. Jenny might or might not know what to do.

Outside, the woman in the blue suit is still fending off wasps and she looks exasperated. I ache to chase away her boyfriend and sit down with her. From that fresh vantage point, I would look inside, see Jenny and not recognize her. I want everything to be different. Change it all the way back. Problem is, I have the nerve for nothing but this, the here and now. I want these changes only because I'm a coward and too many of the futures I envision involve damage to us, real humiliation. I'm like a mole, I realize. Blind, and burrowing deeper.

Barry comes back more ecstatic than I've ever seen a man, practically boiling over with joy. "Okey dokey," he says, rubbing his hands together. "What do you two want to do?"

Well, after we've smacked you around, a good curry would be nice, I think, but keep it to myself.

"Another gin," Jenny says confidently. "And another after that."

Barry nods. "And you? Another pint? Or maybe just a half."

Jenny regards me carefully, like a bus driver trying to decide if I want off at this stop, her foot wavering over the brake.

I say, "Whisky. Big one. And a pint too."

Jenny smiles gently, and I do my best to beam right back, to outshine her. She rests a hand on my leg and very lightly drums a tune on my thigh. We wait like that.

"Don't you just feel so alive?" Jenny gushes.

"I feel endangered," I say, watching the door.

Jenny says, "Same thing."

She seems to pout for a second, then she squeezes my leg hard where the muscle feeds into the knee. I shoot up from my stool like a rocket; a beer-spraying yelp escapes me.

"How about now?" she laughs, raising her glass. "You feel alive now?"

Barry tries to join in the festivities. He looks about furtively, then pulls himself the better part of a pint. I watch him knock the bottom of his glass against Jenny's gin. "Cheers," he says.

But Jenny ignores him completely. Then she changes her mind. "Shove off," she says.

I reach for my beer. "I think I felt something there," I say.

"Was it good?"

"Not bad," I say. "Try it again."

"Shove off," she says, imitating Barry's fake accent.

Barry taps at his watch. "Less than ten minutes, my friends," he says, bitter again, his eyes dark.

Jenny passes a hand back and forth in front of her face. "Tick-tock, tick-tock."

Lionel wakes up and lifts his head a few inches from the bar. I see the woodgrain imprinted on his cheek. "Neanderthal," he slurs.

"Good one," I tell him. "Bang on. You hear that, Jenny?"

"Neanderthal," Jenny says, in as deep a voice as she can muster. She slides easily off her stool and hops about like a monkey, scratching her armpits.

"You feel alive yet?" she says, leaning in for her gin, her red lips looming wet. "I do it all for you, you know."

I nod at her furiously, my nerves buzzing. But at the same moment I realize nothing has really changed for me, because all I can think is: six minutes left, or Christ, maybe only five.

Whole World

A siren dopplers by the house, the wail fixed atop a blur of police car. After that it's a fire truck, chased by a mud-splashed ambulance. I'm on the porch, twelve years old, dipping a wire O into a syrupy green mix of detergent and tap water. Each wave of my arm releases a string of iridescent, jiggling bubbles. The whole world's in every one of them, but inverted, convex.

Even over the scream of traffic I can hear my grandfather indoors, yelling. The hot August air is moving voices as easily as it lifts my procession of soapy balloons over the neighbour's green volleyball net, a mesh strung loosely between two bent white saplings. Grandfather is watching the wrestling again. Every Saturday afternoon he pulls his well-worn canary yellow La-Z-Boy a little closer to the TV for the one o'clock start.

Before coming outside I watched it with him for a while. We cheered on Jack Winston, a three-hundred pound circus strongman, as he battled Bulldog, a real madman from Timmins who hasn't shaved in four years. Winston grabbed Bulldog's foot-long red beard and spun him around the ring. Bulldog ran like mad trying to keep up with his chin. By then Grandfather was perched on the very edge of his seat, totally immersed. He hiked his pant legs up a few inches so they didn't pull as much at the knees. His white shins are peppered with liver spots, the skin scaly as a fish's; his calf muscles droop sac-like at the rear. He clapped his hands repeatedly, hooting and hollering, all the while wiping wild getaway strings of spit from his chin. When I told him I was going outside he merely flapped a loose-skinned hand dismissively; his eyes never left the television.

But the sirens eventually register with him. I hear his foot-steps on the stone tiles in the front hall.

"What's all the racket out here, Buddy?" He rests a warm hand on my head and messes my hair. I get a whiff of the cherry-scented tobacco that has settled on his skin and in his grey cardigan, patched at the elbows with rough brown suede.

I turn and squint, the sky behind him blinding, a cobalt blue. "Wrestling over, Grandfather?"

"Commercials," he says, shaking his head and peering seriously down the street. "So were they heading towards town or away?"

"Away," I tell him.

"Hell of a racket, eh? You could wake the dead." He scratch-es at his stubbled chin. "I suppose that would come in handy, though, wouldn't it?"

I smile awkwardly and stir my potion. A dozen slick new orbs cluster on its forest-green surface, reflect our two upside-down faces over and over.

I'm at his house today because my grandmother has been in hospital the last week and my parents are worried. "Your grand-father needs company," my dad explained. "We don't want him dwelling on things too much. Your grandma will be fine, we know she will, but while we're at the hospital maybe you can cheer him up."

"But why isn't Grandfather going to the hospital?" I asked.

My mother looked at me cautiously. "It's hard on him, that's all. They upset each other. You don't want your grandad get-ting sick now, do you?"

The surgeons at Hotel Dieu have replaced one of the valves in my grandmother's heart. It was a difficult operation for an old woman to endure. One doctor said it was like being hit by a bus, and when she first awoke Gran had no idea where she was, didn't even recognize her husband. She was convinced all the doctors were mafiosi. They had kidnapped her for her savings, and probably for at least one of her kidneys. No one, she said, was allowed to touch her. My grandfather was pretty rattled.

"What if she never comes back?" he asked, hunched over a plastic table in the cafeteria.

My mother tried to calm him. "She'll be fine, Dad. It's just a natural disorientation from the anaesthetic."

Grandfather waved a frightened finger. "There's nothing natural about this. Nothing whatsoever! You hear me?"

Next morning Gran was a little better. Her room had a high window looking over the lake. A hundred anglers were assembled along its shore for the start of the salmon run; the rowing team from the university skimmed past like a many-legged bug. We related this scene to her, described it vividly enough that she cooed, *How lovely, my dears. Oh I do look forward to seeing that so much.* Her optimism was reassuring, but it alarmed me to realize that beneath the orange afghan comforter and the pink flannel nightgown that reached to her ankles, under the gauze bandage and sterile wrap, lurked a foot-long bristling canyon of stitches. Even more frightening was the notion that somewhere on that tired muscle the surgeons had attached a new piece of tissue, and my grandmother's blood, once every time through the body, now flooded into her heart through the transplanted gristle of a recently slaughtered pig.

I can hear the wrestling inside the house. Grandfather checks his watch, taps on the scratched glass, and then stares down the street as if he can see right through the two-storey houses along Coronation Boulevard, all the way to Bath, to Millhaven, wherever the sirens were headed. For several minutes I watch him, notice how his eyes become at a certain moment glassy and immobile. I know he is probably thinking about the hospital, envisioning the operating room, his wife's narrow white chest pried open with terrifying steel tools, her heart quivering like a nearly drowned bird in a congested bloody pool. A hissing plastic mask over her mouth and nose. That is what *I* see, anyway, fluttering at the back of *my* eyes; every bit as real, as potent as anything in the summer gardens all around me. But I say, "She'll be fine," and tug at his woollen sleeve. "Maybe she'll even get out today." Grandfather nods. But, just as he did with the wrestling, he remains focussed on the world directly in front of him and avoids looking at me.

When she was healthy, Gran often led me enthusiastically through this garden, prim in her spotless black rubber boots and floral-print gloves, pointing out lily of the valley and morning glory, explaining the differences between deciduous and evergreen. Afterwards she would make lunch and pour herself a little Bristol Cream, which she sipped on most of the afternoon. Recently, though, she had mostly rested, sprawled in an Adirondack armchair my parents positioned deep in the shade of a rustling silver birch. From there she gestured limply out across her slowly declining half-acre.

"There are snapdragons down around the compost," she said. "And I bet you didn't know this, but they get a drug from them that I take every day for my heart. It's deadly poison if you get too much. But a little now and again..." She trailed off into silence, tears welling, both lips trembling, and half-gone ice cubes rattling in a timidly held glass of iced tea.

Grandfather and I shift slightly on the porch as two boys about my age burst shrieking from next door. They dance about in gym shorts and matching scarlet T-shirts that read *Ted's Plumbing Supplies*. They lob a scuffed leather soccer ball back and forth over the volleyball net, then laugh girlishly and run in tight dizzying circles. I wave my bent-wire wand and send a bright stream of bubbles cruising towards them. The taller of the boys glares, mutters something about distraction. *How are people supposed to concentrate?* he wonders. He smacks at a descending bubble and it explodes softly in his face. Other see-through globes settle on the lawn around the net; each one vanishes in a discreet spray of droplets. The boys make a sudden game of it, chase around the yard, stomping dramatically, leaping into the air and knocking perfect rounds from the sky, throwing their harder ball to intercept my delicate wavering creations.

Grandfather scowls energetically at these destructive young athletes. And then, when I blow a dozen more glassy spheres their way, he scowls at me too. I stop, embarrassed without knowing why. I am aware of the television again. It sounds as if the crowd is cheering a new gladiator. The cheap terrible noise fills the trees, gets caught in the neighbour's net like a school of fish, and my bubbles seem like oxygen rising through this too-blue ocean.

In the distance a siren again. And then the muddied ambulance careens and screams back down the street. When it has passed I see that Grandfather has his hands over his ears, his eyes screwed shut.

A couple minutes later and a Jetta swoops into the driveway. I jump up but Grandfather stays rooted to the porch.

"Dad! Dad! How's Gran?" I squeal.

My father climbs slowly from his car in his rumpled chinos, untucked denim shirt, and flashes a thin-lipped smile I can't interpret one way or the other. He drums lightly on the roof of the car, then reaches back inside for a newspaper. Teasing me. Finally he says, "She's going to be okay, son. What did I tell you?" His smile broadens and he waves the paper towards the house. "Hello there, Dad."

My grandfather mumbles something I don't catch. Then he picks up my jar and extracts the dripping metal ring. He blows delicately through its centre. A bubble begins to form but then retreats. He tries again. The liquid stretches trembling into a sphere the diameter of a child's head. It breaks free tentatively and drifts to the lawn, too heavy, it seems, to float away. It bounces once, twice. But then, rather than bursting, it rises into the air. Grandfather points at the two boys playing in its path. "Don't you dare touch it," he warns. He steps gingerly down onto the grass where he can watch his creation move around the side of the house; his eyes are brighter than I have seen them all day. "You be sure to let that one go, boys. You hear me?"

Shooting the Breeze

I've worked eight ten-hour shifts in a row, and my sanity is a big question mark. So when Keith Chiasson comes in doing his "Hey, it's the happy bartender" routine, I'm none too receptive. "Someone in your family die?" he says boisterously, sliding onto a bar stool. "Man, you look miserable." He points lazily at the Moosehead tap. "Hit me."

I pour his pint a couple of ounces short. It looks nice, has a big creamy head, but wait a couple of minutes. Let it settle. Watch it shrink into the glass. When I put the lager down Keith grins, tugs with a couple of dirty fingers at the corners of his mouth. "Do this in front of a mirror every day," he suggests. "Get the muscles in your face used to the movement. A few months it'll be natural."

Keith thinks he's God's gift to stand-up, but coming face-to-face with me makes him insecure, throws a wrench into his small-screen picture of the world. I lean over his Moosehead. "It's wearing a bit thin," I say quietly.

He shifts uncomfortably, the battered captain's chair swivelling and creaking beneath him. Problem is, Keith heads up the Foot and Mouth dart team, and this is a pub that's seen better days. You take what you can get, the boss says, and apparently what we get is shit like Keith. Half-baked morons who drop in for a cheap pint on their way home from work at the paint factory.

"What do you mean?" he snivels, reddening. He's worried, but trying to come across indignant. His eyes are all over the place, but I'm so close that I fill up his whole world.

"Means I'm close to the breaking point, Keith. Bastards like us, you never know when we might snap. Best to keep your mouth shut for a bit." I flash a big shit-eating grin and walk away, fiddle needlessly with the tape in the cash register. Happiest I've felt all night.

About eleven, Mike Higgis drops in to complain about the failure of his latest relationship. He sounds like a broken GI Joe doll, a frayed string in his back, voice rising piteously at the end of every sentence. But tonight, when I've made less than ten bucks and the cryptic crossword has me stumped, I'm fairly pleased to see him.

Mike and I lived together for a while back in the eighties. He was dealing a lot of hash and I was using prettily heavily. Things worked out fine until I put the moves on one of his old girlfriends, Heather something. Mike got it into his head that I had "fucked with the karma." I told him nothing had happened but he swore at me, jabbing heavily at his temple. "In your head it happened. In your skull it fucking well happened." Fair enough. Three weeks later I was gone, cleared off to the Yukon for the summer. I climbed Grey Mountain, sat up there drinking gin with a woman who managed a health food store in Whitehorse and another guy, a copywriter from Brazil. I never did tell Mike how one night Heather and I had ended up on one of the apartment's deep stone window ledges, our backs braced against opposite walls, bare legs entwined, my eyes fixed on her thighs and transported by the way she would occasionally rub her hands over them as if to wipe away the film left by my looking so hard. We stayed that way for an hour, until I began to slur the memories I produced for her. She laughed at me, then swung giddily and playfully away. For what seemed like another hour I watched her lean over the kitchen counter waiting on the kettle, steam swallowing her face, her pale neck and shoulders.

Mike wants to know if I can buy him a beer. Keith has moved away to the dartboard and is throwing underhand, never putting his pint down. Once in a while he looks over and nods, as if there's a bond between us, as if my telling him to shut the fuck up has created a new mutual respect. I slide Mike a Carlsberg and he spins a buck over the bar.

I figure I may as well get him started. "Trouble in paradise?" I say.

Mike nods, gnaws at the inside of his cheek, and I wonder whether he's stoned. I expect him to launch into a diatribe about how badly he's been treated, but instead he goes off on a tangent about Kuwait and the time his father spent teaching physics there. He has a few good stories about this part of his life: doing H in school, the back row of class, taking turns to nod off; drinking moonshine on the 52nd floor of a jet black apartment building full of diplomats and professors, the parking lot crammed with cream-belted cops who didn't know what to do. Tonight, though, he talks about table tennis, how good he is at it because in the desert there's fuck all to do: "Me and two Arab engineers used to play on a scarlet table in the basement of a shoe store," he says. "When people look at me, they might not automatically see a natural player. But I could thrash most of them."

"I played in England," I tell him enthusiastically. "I was pretty good."

"I'd whip your ass," Mike says and laughs as if it's the funniest thing he's ever said. And right then it is pretty damned humorous — two guys in a puke-stinking bar on the edge of a glacial lake bragging about ping-pong skills they honed on the other side of the world.

"I highly doubt it," I say aggressively. Mike's almost on the floor. "You piss yourself and you're out of here," I tell him.

Keith regards us sadly from beneath the spotlights aimed at

the dartboards. I imagine he wonders why he can't make me laugh like that. I tell Mike what happened earlier and he says, "I bet he feels about this tall," and holds his thumb and forefinger about an inch apart. He aims the illustration in Keith's direction. "I squish you, little bug boy," he says in his best B-movie scientist voice, all German menace and cartoon timbre.

"So what about Julie?" I offer, thinking I'd rather he launch into it now than hang around until four in the morning.

He repeats her name, shaking his head, as if the word came in a dream and he's yet to make sense of it. "Julie." He shakes his head.

"Is it over?" This vocabulary, I realize, hasn't changed since we were sixteen.

"Think so," Mike says, and swallows the last of the Carlsberg. He pushes the glass towards me and I fill it halfway.

"Apparently," he says, "I insulted her brother. And Julie says her family is far too close-knit to put up with that sort of thing. 'My ancestors were persecuted,' she says to me, 'and my generation will be different.' *Persecuted*, I say, *what the fuck am I doing that persecutes you.* 'Well, you're on the road to it,' she says. 'Laughing at someone is almost there as far as I'm concerned.'" Mike wags a finger at me. "And this, if you can believe it, is in the middle of a perfectly good dinner: leg of lamb, new potatoes, mint sauce, apricot something or other in the oven. You get the picture?"

"Not really," I confess. "Where did it happen? I didn't know Julie had a brother."

"Toronto. Last weekend. We took in a Jays game, a couple of flicks at the Carlton. Everything was hunky-dory until Sunday Brunch. She takes me to this Victorian house in Cabbagetown. Big place. We pull up outside and she says, 'We're having lunch with my brother.' Springs it on me."

I shake my head. The pub is still pretty much empty. I grab a rag and make as if I'm wiping down the bar.

"Anyway," Mike says, "this pudgy little guy opens the door. Not ugly, but his hair was almost gone and he was white. Shit, he was the least sunned man I have ever seen. Worried me, I thought maybe he had cancer or AIDS, you know? Some disease that keeps him indoors. But he had a healthy appetite, and he was amiable enough. I liked him is what it boils down to. And what's more, he looked familiar. I'm sitting across the table from him and I'm thinking, *Where the hell have I seen you before?* Finally I twig to it. You remember that beer commercial where they're in court because some asshole has dared complain that the beer, whatever brand it is, isn't the best brew in the world? Guy gets exiled to Alaska for uttering such trash. You remember that one?"

I shrug. "Vaguely."

"Well, this guy's the prosecuting attorney. I'm sure of it. Only he denies it, says he hasn't acted since university. Thing is, the more I think about it, the more sure I am. The way he moves, everything. Especially now I've got him riled up a bit and he's got to defend his position. But he won't have any of it. Eventually I laugh and say, *Hey, don't sweat it. Beer ads are nothing to be ashamed of.* I tell him John Travolta got his start in deodorant commercials and look at him now. *Come on*, I say, *let's put the TV on. A celebrity in the family, that's great.* Well, Julie gets right pissed off, tells me I shouldn't accuse her brother of lying. 'You only just met him, for Christ's sake,' she says. So I back off. I ask him: *What do you do?* This is as we attack dessert — which, by the way, was absolutely fucking incredible. Some Spanish woman comes in once a week and cooks up a bunch of meals for him. Man, I'd like her address. But Jack is real vague: 'Oh, I do this and that,' he says. 'Not much right now. Nothing you'd be interested in.' That sort of bullshit. *This is a pretty fancy place for a guy who doesn't do much right now*, I say. *Unless, of course, you just got paid a shitload by the beer company to do that ad.* I'm trying to be funny, you know, but Julie freaks. Jack tries to calm her down, tells her it's okay, I'm a funny guy, he's not offended. But she goes ballistic. Next thing you know I'm on the train back here. Far as I know she's still there."

"You seen the commercial since you got back?"

"Nope. It's weird. I keep looking for it. Last week it was everywhere, now I can't find the damn thing. I was up until three this morning looking for the fucker. It's like he pulled some strings and took it off the air."

"Yeah, that's what you need," I tell him. "A good conspiracy theory to round out your week."

"Oh I know it's bullshit, but I just want to know one way or another. I mean, why would a guy lie about that sort of thing?"

"It's a world-class mystery, Mike." I shake my head like I'm completely dumbfounded.

About then, Patti Hollingsworth walks in. I haven't seen her in ages. She used to drag me everywhere to see this band her brother played in, The Lemming Meringues. *It's so clever*, she used to say. Their music bored me, the singer's predictable hysterics, but I tagged along because I got to see Patti dance, all loose-limbed and free of any inhibitions. She recognizes me before I have time to decide which way to play it. Seeing her is a shock. I thought she had moved down to the States, was doing some architectural work for the Olympic Committee in Atlanta. Mike realizes something is going on and looks over his shoulder. "Patti," he exclaims. "Comment ça va?"

Patti looks puzzled and it's obvious she's running his face through the Rolodex. "Mike!" She throws her arms around his shoulders and winks at me.

Turns out Patti designs ships now, and some Marine work-shop I never heard of is building one of her designs for the Coast Guard. "It's right down the street," she says, pointing through a wall, trying to orient herself. "Down by the brewery. You'd know it if you saw it. I flew up to supervise the final details."

"Flew up?"

"I'm in California. Got to be near the water. Strictly business, you understand." She laughs easily.

"I was thinking of you the other day," I lie.

"Oh yeah?"

"Yeah. There's a guy lives near me who walks his ferret by the house. He wears the same outfit every day: beat-up penny-loafers, cream sport socks, blue plaid shorts, undershirt and a stained Homburg."

"And?"

I shake my head. "It's his ferret, see." Patti squints sceptically, puts a hand on a hip. "The way it moves through the grass like a Slinky." I say. "Like a creamy wave through the green ocean grass. Actually, though, I can never figure out whether that diving weasel is the boat, its toothy prow, or the wave. Foreground or background. It's a mesmerizing sight. I think you'd appreciate it."

"Maybe." Patti nods seriously, then grins. "And absolutely wild that you would think of me in that situation, considering I only just told you I do the boat design work. Prescient of you. Some would say supernatural."

I stammer something about it being the architectural details of the scene that made me think of her. "Gaudi's curves," I say. "You know how organic he is. The ship stuff, that's just coincidence." But I'm completely screwed.

Patti touches my hand. "It's okay," she says, and I feel about ten years old; less than half the age I need to be to talk to a woman who designs ships and flies in from California. Patti says she wants to shoot some pool and saunters away with a double gin and tonic.

"Maybe she'll find your dishonesty endearing," Mike says. "Or maybe you can just get her drunk."

An hour later I head downstairs for a case of Blue. When I come back up she's left. "A coincidence," Mike says. "Don't read anything into it. She was going to wait, but thought you might be gone for ages. Said to blow you a kiss. Or maybe it was just to blow you. Too bad you weren't here to clear that one up."

By the time I've got everyone out it's almost two. The streets are quiet. A roadsweeper groans down by the water. A car in the multi-storey parking lot next door sloshes through a puddle on the top deck. I've heard that the cops sit up there and talk. If they get bored they take their hats off and stand at the edge spitting on the drunks walking home. I figure it can't possibly be true if so many people are saying it. At least not any more; the higher-ups would have put a stop to it. I head for the hospital.

My sister's on Connell Six. Depression is getting the better of her. Prozac worked for a while. Then it was Zoloft, Luvox, and some older shit that made her sweat, made her stay up nights wondering if she had the nerve to end it all, tamping down the urge to toss herself off the balcony and twist to the ground like a leaf. Now the shrink has decided to bring her in for two weeks of observation; he wants to try out a new high-dose treatment. Normally I'd be mighty suspicious of the guinea pig routine, but I've met this guy and he seems to be on the level.

Visiting hours are way over, but the nurses up in psychiatric are a pretty easygoing lot. It's a different world. Most of the people they see are so completely fucked up the usual rules don't apply. Besides, they know what I do for a living, the nightmarish schedule I've got. Most times they just glance up and wave me on through the double doors. Sheila, I know, will be staring out the reinforced floor-to-ceiling windows of the common room. She never seems to sleep. Sedatives slow her down but never quite knock her out. I read once about a security guard in Switzerland. He was hit on the back of the head during a robbery twenty years ago and hasn't slept a wink since. Hell on earth. But then I walk into the salmon-painted room and Sheila's flat out in the recliner, mouth open, snoring. The latest *Entertainment Weekly* is open on her chest, Michelle Pfeiffer's airbrushed face right where my sister's heart should be. I sit in the canary yellow lounger next to hers and stare down at ambulances coming and going for a while, listening to her breathe. *It's the only thing I get right any more*, she told me the other day. Outside the room I hear the rattle of the steel canteen trolley, its two attendants making enema jokes, bum cracks.

Three in the morning, Sheila's still out cold. I begin to won-der if there's something wrong with her, which is ridiculous. Sad to think that if she started acting like the most well-adjust-ed woman in the city I'd be freaked out. If she showed signs of thinking outwardly instead of obsessing all day, or took her kid to a movie, or out for pizza, I'd be completely stunned. We come to expect certain behaviours. The abnormal becomes routine, safer than the unexpected. If Sheila were suddenly well, I would have a nervous breakdown worrying about her.

Her mouth's open and I note the three mercury fillings on the lower left side of her jaw. Then I study the fine, cotton-thread scar on her ring finger. A carrot-topped shit named Michael Bushnell slammed a garden gate on Sheila's hand when she was six years old. Almost took the digit clean off. I remember my grandmother worrying that it was going to ruin Sheila's wedding day, having no finger to put the ring on. But they reattached the finger and Sheila was okay until they tried to remove the cast two months later. She was so panicked by the electric saw that she had to be anaesthetized. It was that or tie her down, which struck everyone as a real cruelty. *Drugs are cheap enough, so put her to sleep*, I guess that was the doctor's opinion. Shame it's not so easy for her any more.

I scribble a note over Michelle Pfeiffer's face — *You look like an angel, She. Couldn't bear to wake you* — and then I tiptoe back into the hall. They've mopped and the floor shines at me, slightly greasy. I leave a trail all the way to the elevator.

Over at the nurse's stand I spy Keith Chiasson, apparently signing some forms. It takes me a minute to clue in. Then I remember. Sheila's told me about someone on the floor named Mary, Mary Chiasson. Apparently she's really messed up, schiz-ophrenic and not responding. Man, if Keith's here at this hour things must be worse. I consider going over and offering sup-port, condolences, whatever's needed, but the elevator arrives with an absurdly bright ping and I dart inside. The noise proba-bly made Keith turn around, he may even have seen me fleeing

— but fuck it. The thought of an alliance, common ground with him, well, it gives me the shivers.

By the time I get down to the third floor, though, I realize that's all there is: a bunch of stories colliding, four billion characters mostly oblivious to each other. Chaos theory. Everything connected to everything else, but in ways our mostly-water brains can't comprehend. I know a guy who worked at the TV station. He used to prattle on all the time about this stuff. Butterflies in the Amazon causing thunderstorms in Toronto. Drove him crazy in the end, but that makes sense: he was the goddamn weatherman. I think he did some time in here too. Then Keith shows up. And Ted Fischer works here. He's a low-rent, coke-dealing asshole I kicked out of the bar. Used to stand around with his pint, talking in see-through code about how many cars he had sold to such-and-such last year. It was obvious he wanted me to know he meant grams of blow. Used the bar phone all the time too. One night I got fed up with it all, the way he stood cracking his knuckles and twisting his gold chains, running spit back and forth over his teeth. Arrogant cocksucker. I told him: *Fuck off, Ted. It's nothing personal, but I don't want you in here.* He threatened me, the usual dark alley stuff, and began smacking his chest with a closed fist, yelling something I took for Japanese. I wanted to laugh, I really did, assuming this was another code supposed to show me he was a martial arts expert. I held open the door and said, *Get the fuck out.* He did, his red mouth full of spit and my heart pounding like a kettle drum. Afterwards, some big black guy got up from his table. Told me, *Ted's an orderly at the hospital, works the morgue mostly. A few months ago he took my boy to the O.R. Calmed him down, did a good job. Weird how much a man can change when he takes the uniform off.*

So anyway, Ted's probably in this anthill somewhere, right now, carting off the dead ones. Everyone else is glued to rented TV sets, watching Mike's friend in that damn beer commercial.

And then there's Patti, the only one who doesn't seem to fit.

Which is undoubtedly why we're not together. She's probably on her way back to California at this very moment. Even though she said she was going to be in town for a few days. I don't buy it. She doesn't belong. And when I get out onto the streets it's ten to one I look up and see her plane streaking south between the stars.

Camera

I'm not in the best of moods as it is, so when the phone rings I think, God help the poor bastard on the other end.

"Peter, it's Jack," he says.

"Jack who?" I ask.

He puffs excitedly. "Yeahyeahyeah." It's a nervous exclamation, meant to show that information is getting through. "I need to get my camera back," he says. "The light outside, you seen it? Wow!"

"Well it's too goddamn late," I bluff, an image in my head of his ancient large-format Hasselblad. "I gave you a week, man. What did you think, that I'd provide indefinite storage for that monstrosity?"

Jack isn't sure how to take me, I can tell. His attachment to this camera is unnaturally severe. I don't think machines, devices, should assume that much importance in a person's life, however good the lens is, however aesthetically pleasing the chassis.

"Heh heh," he offers grimly. I sense him switching the receiver from one hand to the other, sitting up straighter in the leather lounger he keeps near his front window. "Seriously, can I come by and pick it up?"

"Sold it, man. Seriously."

"Heh heh."

"Really." I nod furiously, knowing full well I can do some permanent damage here. If I want to push it that far. Which I do. Sort of. I mean, really, what a dumb fuck. He trusts me enough to leave a four-thousand-dollar camera here while he's off on some wildlife assignment. But right now he's ready to believe I'd fence the damn thing. I'm offended. Deeply, deeply hurt.

"What did you get for it?" Jack says as jovially as he can, trying to play along.

"Uh, three pints of Guinness and some lasagna."

"Good pints, were they?"

"It was pouring well, Jack," I tell him, trying lamely for an Irish accent. "Otherwise I'd have held out for more. Some whisky maybe."

He laughs, a bit relieved, and I join in. For a few seconds we bust up the connection.

"No. Hold on a sec," I say. "I've got it wrong. It was four pints. Aye. There was a woman other end of the bar I bought one for. Not often you find a woman who likes to put away the black the way she did."

"A real beauty, then?"

I shrug. "Sure," but then I let silence swamp us. Make him work for it, I think. After all, my dog, Sadie, shit all over the cream carpet while I was out today. Then walked through it. It doesn't matter how good your camera is, there's no making that look pretty. It fouls your day.

"How's seven?"

"Seven what?" I ask, knowing exactly what he means.

"To come by. Seven o'clock. Tonight."

"No good."

"Why?"

"Busy, man."

"What's with this *man* shit?" Jack says. "You stoned? Sarah bring some dope over? Is that what's going on here? You want me to call back later?"

"I broke it, Jack." I say solemnly. "I'm sorry."

A silence, then: "The camera?"

"Yes, the camera."

"Don't screw around, Peter, okay? I mean, a joke's a joke. I can appreciate the humour here, but leave it alone now. The Hasselblad's fine, right?"

I ask him, "You get this worried about Marnie?"

"What?"

"Marnie. Would you be this excited if you thought something had happened to your wife? A little fender bender, maybe?"

"Fuck off, Peter. Fuck right off."

The line goes dead.

That asshole, I think. That sanctimonious bastard. As if he's above a good laugh. But I've really pissed him off. Nothing irreparable of course, because I'll pull a self-pity thing. Make up some personal trauma that made me act this way. Get forgiveness and sympathy.

I hang up the phone and peer down the dim hall towards the back room. A yellow stain, probably permanent, the shape of Wales on the carpet. I lean my head on the wall and the phone rings again, right in my ear: it scares the shit damn near right out of me, which would make me a hypocrite for cursing the dog.

"Yeah, Jesus," I yelp into the handset, heart thumping.

"You *were* kidding, right?"

It's him again.

"Jackie!" I say. "The Righteous One, the Man with the Perfect Eye. Calling me back."

"Well *weren't* you?"

"No sir," I say. "Dropped it. The Hassel Man tumbled. It broke in two. Lens popped right out on the carpet, bounced, hit a spike on my golf shoe, took a big chip off. Neat rainbow effect if you hold it up to the light, though."

"Why did you pick it up?" Jack whines.

"Cleaning, man. Just doing some dusting; you know, getting a handle on my space."

"You are messed up."

"Nope. Stone-cold sober." I wind the black phone cord around my hand, pull it tight to create a blood-free zone under my fingernails.

"I'm coming by."

"Wait a few days, Jack. I know a guy who says he can do wonders with glass. Re-grind it for you. Fixes a lot of sunglasses in his spare time."

Jack hangs up on me again.

Well screw you too, I think. I pop open a beer and flop on the couch. The plan now is to watch *The Simpsons* until he arrives. That'll set a mood. I take off my shirt so I'm in a singlet just like Homer's. I pour a couple ounces of beer on myself. Puff out my stomach, inflate it like they would for surgery. All I need is some hair on my shoulders.

Yeah, that's what I need. More hair.

Twenty minutes and the sonofabitch hasn't arrived. He lives a mile away. On his hands and knees he could have crawled here by now. I search out his camera. Take it gingerly, respectfully, out of its carrying case. I put my eye to the viewfinder and aim out the window. Just then Jack turns his Toyota into the driveway and I snap a picture of the arrival. Beautiful, I think. Blurred by speed, trails of red tail lights. Magic.

I hold the Hasselblad out in front of me and drop it casually to the floor. I pick it up and shake it like a tambourine. No loose parts. I aim for where the floor meets the wall and drop it again. But more forcefully, giving gravity a hand. The doorbell rings and I launch the dying thing underhand at the wall.

Jack's face appears in the window. He must be standing right in the flower beds. Size elevens all over the daffodils. He presses his nose to the glass and peers in at me. He's grown a beard. I'll be damned, he's a wild man. Look at those eyes.

I cry out and point at him. "Look Jack, look! There's a yeti in the garden. You should get a picture of this."

Jack puts both hands flat against the glass and I consider that he might push, break through to my side. But he doesn't, he just watches me pointing at him.

"Jack, Jack, look at your poor camera." I pick up the remains and display them in the palms of my hands. "Your baby," I moan. "Cry for me, Jack, cry."

I move to the window, stand in front of him. A prisoner before his visitor. I bring the camera up to eye level. The black and silver dove, its unblinking eye. Jack regards it briefly, then stares only at me. For an instant I see my own reflection super-imposed over his face and I understand what he must be think-ing. Then it's gone.

I take a step backwards. I lower my hands, pause and swing them abruptly forwards. "Leave the nest now," I murmur, "leave the nest," and watch the heavy bird clatter away. The window drops in ragged sheets to allow the camera's passage. The world falls apart for both of us.

Piker

I'm feeling pretty fucked, no question. Every few seconds it's like I'm levitating, turning into a real David Copperfield. But this is no sleight of hand, there's no dark wagon parked outside with a ton of polished mirrors. Maybe it's not my whole body that's lifting, just my head, or something in my head, separating slightly, deciding it's had enough and wanting to rise above it all. Out of this shit. I can't say I blame it really. So go on, get out of here, vamoose! The last thing I need right now is a preoccupation with metaphysics, a mind-body split messing with me.

I'm in this real shithole sports bar. The place is deserted, which is no surprise since it's not even seven o'clock yet. And I'm drinking Rickard's, a piss-poor beer dressed up fancy if ever I saw one. This is maybe my third pint so (tick-tock tick-tock) I must have got here five-ish, I suppose. What's fascinating me is these twelve display cases above the bar. They look like TV sets with the guts removed. You've got the wooden box and the convex glass screen, but nothing else of the original. (Somewhere out back there's probably a pile of smashed tubes and plastic knobs numbered zero to thirteen.) And every one of them contains a stuffed bird. On the left it's a half-plucked or moulting mallard. Above the wine glass rack it's something

Chinese, gold-crested and mangy. I can tell it's Chinese, or supposed to be, because of the paint-by-numbers pagoda on the back wall of the case. There are also a couple of motley black numbers that look like they were related, brother cormorants maybe, or shags. Survivors of an oil spill. Survivors? What the fuck am I saying? Look at them! Do they look like survivors to you? Anyway, at the end, in the shade over the cash register, that must be a great horned owl, ears like Prince Charles, Mr. Spock. Feather coat like a sharp tweed suit. Seems to me there were pike up there once too. A different display, I guess. Maybe there's a travelling circus of stuffed animals and these are just on loan. I picture a library at the taxidermist's where you can sign out woodpeckers, nightjars, instead of Tolstoy and Kafka.

I can't concentrate. I'm scattered, thoughts are going out of me like hail, tracer bullets. Right now it's my mother's face, for fuck's sake, and how it takes on some mighty odd twists when she remembers her dad coming home drunk from places just like this. Sometimes he would stagger in the door with a fresh-killed rabbit. It looked small, she says, like a warm glove in his huge hands. That's a created memory I bet, a pretty exaggeration on my mum's part. He said he drank to relax, didn't ever mean to hurt anyone with his absence. He sighed a lot, like he was forever sad to leave the pub. Slurred: *Here, I bought thish from Jacko, he got three today. Hiss new snares mus really be payin off. I'll skin it for you.* The bowie knife slashing viciously through the room's liquored air.

When his wife died she was riddled through with cancer like buckshot, lay on the sofa the last few weeks a skin bag of shit and stuff going rotten. He moved into a bird's-egg-blue mobile home, travelled the world six months of the year. Saw his son in America, flew over the Grand Canyon. Came next to Canada, told Mum he'd given up the bevy altogether; cried it was taking his memories away.

Anyhow, screw it. Makes me shake my head, that stuff. Not why I'm here, no sir. Change the goddamn subject.

You know the weirdest thing about this place? The animal

display cage in the bathroom is empty. Manager says it put too many guys off their game, if you know what I mean. Caused line-ups. But he won't be more specific. Not much left to play detective with, either. No stray hair fragments, or DNA sequences for the forensically ambitious boozer. Just a backdrop of muddy river bank, a gnarled root of alder, grey nettles fringing turquoise sky. It's like you taped a nature show and paused it at the wrong moment, right after the rarest beast in the world took off. River rat's my guess. Or badger. Mean-looking bastards they are sometimes. Must've been pretty dramatic, though, for men to dry up completely in its presence, get so humbled like that.

Four-Gallon Ice Cream, Ten-Gallon Hat

When the waitress dropped off our bill, drawing it like a small pistol from the front of her apron, she let it flutter tableward instead of placing it near us. Geoff deciphered the name scribbled brightly under the blue ink happy face before he looked at the total. He'd been flirting with her for an hour. She was pretty enough, but seemed lazy and rude. "You're out of your mind," I said. "Her?"

Geoff waved the bill under his nose like a paper fan. "Cameo. What do you think of that?"

"What?"

"Cameo. That's her name."

"You're kidding."

"Here. Look."

I took the paper from him and tried to read Candy or Candice, Camara, even, into the royal blue scrawl, but Geoff was right. "Probably an alias," I said. "Like down at the Mexican place where everyone is Wrangler or Buck."

Geoff laughed. "No, no, no. Hold on." He closed his eyes then opened them again sharply: "I've got it. She's telling us her real role in life lies elsewhere; this is just a *cameo* role, this waitress gig."

"She doesn't seem cut out for much more than this, though. There's your problem."

"You're a cruel man," Geoff tutted, pushing his chair back and throwing down a twenty.

On the way out, winding through the obstacle course of chairs I thought Cameo should have sorted by now, he whispered something in her ear. She giggled and threw her hair around. For a second her tray angled precariously over another customer. Then Geoff — preposterously, I thought — winked at her.

"Jesus," I said outside. "You're like a fucking monkey. A pocketful of old tricks and you've got to play with them all."

"Hey." Geoff shrugged. "What can I say?"

I hadn't known him long then. Months, not years. He was a biology student "slumming it" in the first-year film course I was tutoring. The first few weeks I thought he was a fool, a cocky know-it-all with no real interest in learning. And one night in the student pub I told him as much. Most of my group had trudged there through October sleet after a screening of *Blade Runner*, but by midnight only Geoff and I remained.

"Well," he said, momentarily stunned. "But...this is your first time teaching, right?"

I put my pint down carefully, a little drunk. I told him it was.

"Well, there's your answer."

He sounded pleased, his exclamation drifted easily into the rest of the room. He sat up straight.

I looked at him, puzzled.

"You're taking yourself way too seriously," he said. "Buying into the status thing. You should relax."

"Is that what I'm doing, buying into the status?" I considered telling him to fuck off, and then thought about failing all his essays. C-minuses, D-pluses. My throat hurt. Geoff just grinned. I waited but he didn't say anything.

"We should go," I told him. "Or I should, anyway. Lots of work to do, you know?" I emptied my glass.

"I've pissed you off?"

"Somewhat, yeah."

"I'm sorry."

"Why?" I demanded.

"Why not?"

I laughed sarcastically and shook my head as professorially, as sagely, as I could, and then staggered out alone.

The next day Geoff told me I'd left half a pitcher of beer behind. "You're getting old," he crowed. "What a waste. Imagine if I hadn't been there. The waitress would have laughed. 'Poor old man,' she'd say. And did you see her? This is not the sort of woman you want bad mouthing you. Very authoritative, if you know what I mean."

I hadn't got a clue, but his thrilled tone had me grinning furtively into my backpack, rifling through books I didn't need. He was probably my age, maybe a year younger, but I felt like a father grinning at a son's first rude joke.

His work in class improved through the autumn. He was smarter than most of the kids I'd been assigned. He knew without being taught that a film was more than just a story, and he helped out in class discussions, rescuing me when things stalled by suggesting the outrageous, the dubious ("Bergman needed prozac; Belmondo's a fag"). I came to rely on him. And eventually — it must have been almost Christmas — I came to like him.

We were in the same bar one night. I was reading in a tattered red velvet booth near the dart boards. It seems so pretentious to me now, looking back, a man reading Eisenstein, Bazin, the latest Amis, and smoking Camels, in a bar. But it seemed natural back then, I never gave it a thought. My apartment was dingy, cold; where else would I be? And I justified my pint-a-day habit in the exalted name of academia. I kept all the receipts (a frightening number of them), figuring I could claim the beer on my tax return. But when April rolled around I backed away from the idea. I had a persistent vision of the auditor pointing at my scribbled figures, asking if I seriously expected him to believe that a particular pint of Guinness corresponded to chapter three of such and such textbook.

"You busy?"

I looked up and it was Geoff, loaded down with last-minute shopping, an immense green scarf wrapped four, five times around his neck, like a boa constrictor, snow on his ski gloves. I gestured at my book.

"That a yes?" he said.

I thought about it for a second. "I suppose not. What's up?"

"Well, the thing is..." An awkwardness I hadn't seen before came over him, an unnatural bendiness at the waist, like a cramp, and a smile that didn't belong on his face, an expression almost spastic.

"Spit it out."

"I could use a hand is all. My arms are killing me. It's just a few blocks."

"To where?"

"My place."

I raised an eyebrow. It was a gesture I'd rehearsed shamelessly in front of the bathroom mirror lately and grown inordinately fond of. It hinted, it seemed to me, at a world-weariness only the truly wise can know. I knew it was a defence mechanism, a security blanket, but I liked it all the same and carted it everywhere. I rationalized that, at worst, if I'd got it all wrong, it would be seen as a forgivable idiosyncrasy, like a bow tie, or a pipe.

"Oh, come on. It's just around the corner for Christ's sake."

"Take a cab."

"I can't"

"Why not?"

"I spent all my money." He moved a little air with the bags.

"What the hell did you buy? It looks like dumbbells."

"Bingo!"

I got up and took the lighter handful, followed him out the door. "Not trying to pick me up, are you?"

"Don't flatter yourself."

I attempted a self-deprecating laugh and came up short.

Geoff, it turned out, was a nanny, an au pair, a live-in baby-sitter for a young law professor and his architect wife. Geoff introduced me as he shouldered through the living room and up the stairs. He never stopped and I had barely enough time to shake their hands. "Nice to meet you. You too. Thanks very much. See you again." That was the extent of it. And no sign of any kids.

Geoff had the third floor to himself: a huge skylit bedroom, four-piece bathroom and a high-tech kitchenette next to a brick chimney. But for all its well-designed charm it still looked, in Geoff's care, like a biology lab. A potent-seeming microscope hunched under a wide bank of fluorescent lights against one wall, a couple pairs of tweezers lay open on the dining table. Glass slides were everywhere, even on the bed, each labelled meticulously in Latin and English. A yellow nylon washing line had been strung across the room, festooned from end to end with photographs: butterfly wings, looping chains of what I took to be cells shot through the microscope's lens, and at the end of the line a black and white print of a pretty woman bent over a sink washing her hair.

"Nice place."

"It does the trick. Over there." He pointed at an empty press-back chair and I piled up the bags. When I stepped away, one bag tipped and three chocolate oranges rolled over the thick green lawn of carpet. "For the nieces," Geoff said. He was pointing at the oranges. "Just to piss my sister off. Give the kids a nice sugar rush." He chuckled and carted the dumbbells into a corner.

"Who's the woman? A girlfriend?" I tapped at the photograph, set it swaying stiffly on the line.

"Maybe."

"Maybe. What does that mean?"

"Means she probably thinks so and I haven't decided yet."

"Oh." I paced around uncomfortably, not sure whether he was going to offer me a drink or just wanted me out. "When do you head out?"

He didn't answer.

"For the holidays. You're going home, right? To your parents?"

"Maybe for a day," he said. "*The* day. I'll be back the 26th.
You should come over." He was in the kitchen area.

"Seriously?"

"Yeah. Meet Hagar. That's her name."

"Ah," I said carelessly, "the fertile one."

He poked his head around a cupboard door. "Come again?"

"Forget it. It's a Christmas thing. Only time of year I can
remember Sunday School lessons."

"That's funny," Geoff said, nodding.

"No, it's..."

"It's okay, really. You might be dead-on. I don't know very
much about her. I think she may be a stripper. On the circuit,
you know? I keep expecting her to be gone when I wake up."

"Wow," I said, liking the sordid edge to the story, feeling a
little jealous. "But you reckon she thinks of you as her
boyfriend?"

"Seems to." He paused, as if running all the events that had
led to this moment through his head. "So, Boxing Day.
Dinner." He was already holding the front door open for me.

"Thanks," I said, not at all sure how I meant it.

I don't remember much of Christmas Day. My own family had
moved away and I didn't have money for the flight out to see
them. I was dating a woman too, Anne, who was finishing up a
Commerce degree, but she'd gone to Montreal. She had
pleaded with me to go with her, tugging at my sleeve like a
child after ice cream. "Please. Pretty please!" But I'd resisted,
lured by the dark beauty of a holiday spent alone.

"For New Year's," I told her, "we'll go out on the town. Or
have dinner with your parents. Whatever you like."

I think I ate omelettes. One for breakfast and another for
lunch. Dinner escaped me completely. My parents called
middle of the afternoon and right after them my sister from
Boston. But that's it. The rest is a fog pierced only by the
occasional Christmas carol on the radio, the smell of drying
turkey somewhere else in the building.

Boxing Day I got nervous around two. Don't ask me why, it didn't make sense. I was pretty good, I thought, in those situations where near strangers gather at a dinner table. Geoff called about five to make sure I was still coming.

"Hagar is going to be here. Did I tell you that?"

"Sure," I said.

"So when are you coming?"

"Hey, it's your party."

"Seven? Seven o'clock? How's that?" He seemed distracted, not all there. I pictured Hagar the AWOL stripper on her knees giving him a blow job, that microscope humming in the background. Geoff, I imagined, was sipping on eggnog as he tried to talk to me. He had his camera on the table. It wasn't a pretty picture.

Hagar met me at the door. Her hair was damp and that spooked me, it was as if she had stepped right out of the photograph. She was taller, though, than I had imagined her (the photo, remember, had her bent over the sink) and she wore make-up, but not much: a little eyeliner, a gloss on her lips. She really was beautiful. A woman, a full-grown mature woman. I was so used to seeing my friends date girls, awkward changelings, but Hagar was nothing like that. I knew immediately she had never been to university. Again, don't ask me how. A prejudice springing from her appearance, I guess, and a surliness, an anger or bitterness in her that I hadn't seen in a long time. She was tomboyish too, in her faded Levi's, the plaid shirt, the filthy hands. She saw me looking at them.

"Holly," she said, and it confused me. I thought it was an introduction, that I'd heard her name wrong. Everything seemed slightly out of whack; it threw me off my game and I remember I stammered "Ian," and probably blushed.

"I get it from the market every year," she said, and motioned for me to take off my coat.

"You get what every year?"

"Holly. It's not rooted or anything, but I plant it in pots, or old tobacco tins, whatever's around. You see?" She grabbed my arm and led me to a coffee table. Half a dozen sprigs of holly stuck jauntily out of two clay pots. I counted seven red berries and I could smell the wet black soil.

"It won't grow, though, right?"

She looked at me as if considering whether to scold me for my lack of imagination. "Of course not. Just look at it."

Geoff was stirring something at the stove but he raised his eyes heavenward while Hagar had her back turned. I wondered if they were fighting. It didn't seem right that he would betray her this way, so early on in the evening. It set things up wrong.

Dinner was a muddled concoction. Some smoked ham, sausage rolls, beets and pickled onions, a loaf of day-old bread (if that's possible on the 26th of December) and a pitcher of gravy no one seemed brave enough to try. Lots of red wine, though, and when that was gone Geoff rummaged in the kitchen and came up with half a bottle of gin. It made conversation easy. Perhaps lighter than Geoff and I would have liked, but I still didn't know him very well and so I took refuge in the weather, some harmless gossip about the faculty. Hagar looked bored, distracted. She was pleasant with us, smiling, occasionally laughing, but I got the feeling she would rather have been on the back of a motorbike somewhere, or running barefoot in the sun. I realized I was shamelessly romanticizing a stranger's life. I stole glances at her, trying to confirm the initial diagnosis of boredom, and I'm pretty sure she thought I was flirting. She grabbed Geoff's hand, forcing him to eat with just one, and then she ran a finger across his forehead and down along the jawline. Geoff looked uncomfortable and I smiled reassuringly.

"How long did you say you two have been together?" I said. It wasn't meant to put Geoff on the spot but seemed to do just that. He backed his chair away from the table and shook his head free of Hagar's finger. He picked up a napkin and wiped mustard from his lips. The stain it left on the white cloth seemed exactly the shape of Florida, the Sunshine State. Or maybe it was Italy.

"Not long enough," Hagar said, "for Geoff to tell me how he

got this." She put a finger up to Geoff's cheek again.

I couldn't see anything. I thought perhaps she meant his tan, because Geoff was always inexplicably dark, but that wasn't it. This woman had a talent, I decided, for putting people on edge. I liked her but I didn't know if that would last. I understood Geoff's reluctance to get involved. I'd have bet good money she didn't have a lot of friends. Geoff looked awkward, almost frightened. A candle on the coffee table spit and we all turned to watch. Shadows from the holly fluttered over the tabletop and walls like bats.

"Was it a car accident?" Hagar said, quietly, as if by whispering she wouldn't invoke too horrific a memory. I looked for a scar but couldn't find one. No dent in his skull either. Geoff squinted irritably, like a man whose unlisted phone number has just been revealed to a room full of strangers.

"When?" I said. I leaned over the centre of the table for a closer look. Geoff retreated into the dark.

"Years ago. Six. Maybe seven."

"I still don't see anything," I told him. "How bad was it?"

Hagar drew her breath in sharply.

"Pretty bad," Geoff said.

I felt like I was at a seance, talking to someone's long-departed father, a ghost.

"They did a good job," Hagar said. "You hardly notice it."

"What?" I was exasperated. "You look perfectly normal to me."

"Thanks very much," Geoff said.

"Your skull, right?" Hagar said. "And your jaw on this side." She rubbed under his chin as if he were a kitten.

"It was fractured, yeah."

"Your skull. Shit." I couldn't believe it. "What, and they did plastic surgery later on?"

Geoff stood up. "You got it. Give that man a cigar."

I whistled. "Wow."

Geoff collected our dishes and padded over to the kitchen sink. "Change the subject while I'm gone, okay?"

"You've got great eyes," I told Hagar.

She batted her lashes.

"That's not what I meant. To see whatever you see in Geoff's face. What is it, an asymmetry? There's no mark."

"Something like that."

She seemed possessive of the talent, if that's what it was, unwilling to go any further. Or maybe she was just protecting Geoff. I shook my head and said wow again. "So what do you do?" I asked.

She seemed to think about it, to ponder a few different answers, and Geoff watched her, one hand on the open refrigerator door, swamped with yellow light. He still doesn't know anything about her, I thought.

Finally Hagar shrugged and said, "Nothing right now." It seemed painful for her and I wished I hadn't asked. Geoff came and stood behind her. He put his hands on her shoulders as if to say, *You don't have to do that again, it's okay.*

"We need more mix," he said. "I'll be right back. There's a Mac's ..."

"I'll come with you," I offered, but I felt instantly guilty, like a conspirator in a plot to get away from her. It was odd. I was second-guessing everything I did. All of us were.

In the cold the street lights buzzed like long-legged insects. The whole world resembled the inside of Geoff's refrigerator. We half-jogged to Mac's Milk, then did the same coming back. I told Geoff that I liked Hagar, but otherwise we were quiet. He seemed uninterested, preoccupied. I assumed he wanted to avoid talking about his accident. So we ran, like two strangers after a train.

Hagar was sprawled on the bed, one arm over her face, a black delta of hair swamping the pillow, her legs akimbo. She had put a cassette on, some near-ambient, vaguely jazzy stuff and I was positive — no kidding — that she was dying.

"Great music," Geoff said. "Good choice. You like this stuff?"

I shook my head and shrugged. "Who is it? Sounds all right."

I don't remember who he said it was. Hagar moved her arm up over her head and looked out at us druggily. I was convinced there was no way she could lift her head off the pillow, but Geoff seemed unconcerned.

"You okay?" I said. I waggled one of her feet. It felt like an overly familiar gesture, one that might have Geoff raising an eyebrow, but I wanted to feel some resistance, some body heat.

"Uh huh."

"That doesn't sound too convincing."

"I'm fine."

And she sounded fine, her voice was strong. She looked angry, though, perhaps because I'd dared to touch her. Maybe I was wrong; she'd just wanted to lie down a minute, believing we would be longer at the store. I reminded myself that I knew absolutely nothing about her, her habits.

"Good. You had me worried for a minute there."

Geoff took a longer look at this woman collapsed on his bed. "What are you doing?"

"Going to sleep."

"Now?"

"Forever."

My heart leapt at this, a skittish salmon fighting torrents of channelled blood. I looked at Geoff and he said, "Forever? I guess Ian and me get the rest of the booze, then." He wasn't taking her seriously.

"Are you okay?" I tugged again, a worried fetishist, at her socked foot.

"Suuuure. No problem." Her arms flapped above the sky-blue duvet for a moment and then fell into a new, impossibly awkward arrangement.

"Hey!" Geoff kneeled on the bed and shook at her shoulders. Hagar looked up at him dreamily, distantly.

"What's up? What did you do?" Geoff struggled back to his feet and grabbed my arm. He was panicked and I remember feeling pleasure at how flustered he was. It was a fleeting sensation, and it makes me feel awful whenever I recall it. I became calmer knowing something was wrong: my uncertainty dissipated.

"What do you have around this place?" I snapped. "Any drugs?"

"Just Aspirin. A few Tylenol 3's." His hands were shaking.

"What did you take, Hagar?" I leaned over her, spoke as if to a child. She smiled, humouring me, and then closed her eyes again. She rolled around the bed as if someone were caressing her and I think Geoff and I both found it erotic. Our conversations afterwards, though, were all limited to the science of it all: the stomach pump, rates of digestion, the fortunate proximity of the convenience store.

"You should see if Bernie can drive us to the hospital," I suggested.

"Oh Christ. I hadn't thought about that. There's no way we can do it without involving them, I guess."

"Not unless you've got a huge suitcase somewhere."

"Fuck."

Bernie came up looking as if he expected the whole third floor to be missing. He wanted to know how much we knew about Hagar. "What's her last name?" He paced back and forth at the foot of the bed and cast frequent glances at the stairs leading down to his ordered life: the fireplace, the storytelling, the kids in their Fleecy-scented pyjamas.

"I don't know." Geoff said.

"Where does she live?"

"Ottawa someplace."

"And you don't know her surname?"

Geoff looked sheepish.

Bernie said, "Damn. Well, okay, let's get her downstairs. Pick her up."

Geoff blushed. I wondered if he had doubts about his ability to lift her or if the notion of carrying a dying woman through the house did it to him. At any rate, he scooped her up along with the duvet and we pulled that away like an endless handkerchief from a magician's sleeve.

Bernie led us into the living room. "A bit too much to drink is all," he said. He eyed the two kids who sat on the floor trying to put a model airplane together, a sleek grey jet. It surprised me. I had hardly talked to Bernie, but expected Afghani slippers and wooden train sets carved by prison inmates to be more his speed. The boys barely looked up, their curiosity already fully engaged. His wife appeared from the kitchen, a steaming mug in her hands, the scent of chocolate.

"Oh my God," she said. "What's going on?"

"We think she took some pills," I said.

"Not mine," Geoff said, like a suspect firming up his alibi.

Hagar moaned and the two children stopped what they were doing.

"Let's go," Bernie said.

Geoff almost dropped her on the driveway. His footing gave way on an icy patch and he staggered two steps then bumped against the car. Bernie chuckled and shook his head. "Put her on the back seat," he said.

"Yeah, pu' me on the back sea'," Hagar moaned. The words dribbled out.

January 4th she disappeared. Everything in Geoff's place smelled of her perfume — as if she'd wiped it down with a soaked cloth. She left a note that said simply, "Don't forget me."

"No fear of that, is there?" said Geoff bitterly. He sat on the bed and waved the note in front of his face like a fan. It was the first time I'd seen him since Boxing Day. He had telephoned middle of the afternoon on the 27th to say Hagar was okay, they'd pumped her stomach and it was a dozen Valium, some wine, that was all. But I already knew this. I had stayed at the hospital until three in the morning; by then the doctors were just waiting for her to liven up a bit. Geoff had obviously forgotten.

"I felt bad not sticking around to the end," I told him.

He said not to worry. Then: "She's been staying here. I thought she was getting her act together."

"What did Bernie say about that?"

"He was okay. Didn't want a tragedy on his conscience, so he decided a few awkward days were bearable, I guess. You know what people are like. Might not ask me back next year, but..."

He trailed away into silence, still flapping the note. He started up again. "I thought I was helping."

"You were. Hell, you probably saved her life."

He laughed and fell back flat on the bed, staring at the ceiling. "Hey, I thought she was fine. If you hadn't been here I'd have let her sleep."

"I don't think that would have killed her either."

I talked him into heading out for a while. "Let's grab a beer," I suggested. "It'll do you good." And that's when Cameo, the waitress, put in her appearance. I'd never seen a man recover so fast from heartbreak. It repelled me and fascinated me, and when we walked away from the restaurant I looked one more time for a scar on his face, a sign that air had somehow got in there, blown some vital pieces around.

In class after that we acted more professionally. As if I'd seen too much of his life. I also had all the Christmas exams to mark. I spent more time with Anne. We even went to Montreal for a weekend. New Year's Eve had been good for us. I had charmed Anne's parents and she hadn't stopped beaming since. But stupidly I took only a pair of sneakers to Montreal and froze my toes so badly on the Friday that Saturday and Sunday we had to stay close to the hotel. It made us both testy, and we came back less rested than we should have been. And there were pretty women everywhere. Women who wouldn't perhaps graduate in three months, as Anne would, with a commerce degree from a respected university, but knock-outs, women who reduced me to a drooling, distracted version of myself.

In May I moved just out of the city, to a village on the St. Lawrence. I bought an old bicycle and rode in for the classes I had to teach. I didn't see Geoff for weeks on end, but I heard that he had moved too. Then, one afternoon, he showed up at the house. I was sitting on the porch, drinking beer and reading the newspaper. Playing the country squire, was how it felt, and Geoff's intrusion set me brooding before he climbed out of his car. I wasn't sure why. Maybe succumbing to the tug of academia meant rejecting alliances with people like Geoff, people who might damage my chances of advancement.

"Hey!" he called. "You're home." I wished I'd been indoors, somewhere he couldn't see me. "You want to take a ride?"

"Where?" I folded the newspaper.

"Can't say."

"Then I can't go."

"Ah, come on. I haven't seen you for ages. Can't work all the time. Or have they got cameras on you up here? Should I stay off the property?"

I smiled out at him weakly.

"Honest. I think you'll get a kick out of this. It'll bring out the cinematic side of you."

We drove north, through difficult farmland and worse conversation, the fields strewn with erratics, the soil on the Canadian Shield thin, balding. Twenty minutes into the drive, Geoff slowed from eighty to fifty. Soon there were five cars lined up behind us, the closest one darting over the white line and back again, the road too damn bendy to try anything stupid.

I looked over at Geoff. "What's the story?"

"It's close."

He hunched a little towards the windshield, both hands gripping the leather steering wheel. He had the eyes, then, of a bird or a criminal.

He pulled off the road just before Westport. A dark cliff towered over us and it felt like we had driven onto a beach. I looked for caves drilled into the rock by surf but discovered only narrow ledges and, spraypainted about fifteen feet off the ground: *Lucy gives good head.*

"Whoever did that went to a lot of effort," I remarked.

"So the road crews can't clean it off," Geoff said matter-of-factly, and I realized he'd already thought it through.

"So, what's the scoop?"

Geoff didn't answer, he just edged along the rockface, dragging a hand over the jutting, razored surface. His arms were bigger than I remembered.

"Hey, you've been using those dumbbells," I said. "I thought they were a gift."

He wheeled around and half-smiled. "I'm trying to improve myself."

A battered pick-up truck honked as it sped by, and Geoff waved nonchalantly. I thought the driver was probably pissed off because we had stopped on a bend. Then it dawned on me. "This is where it happened."

Geoff nodded, his back to me, and I looked for paint scraped onto the rock, for oil stains on the road, bits of metal, signs of a fire. Nothing.

"I hit about here." Geoff fingered the granite delicately, as if still afraid of how it might come at him. "I guess I fell asleep. I bounced off somehow, I must have caught it a glancing blow. And the car ended up over there." He pointed across the road towards bullrushes, swamp. "Good thing it was late at night, no one to collide with."

"Shit," I said, horrified and not sure what Geoff expected of me.

"Yeah. Someone found me crawling along the gravel shoulder, bleeding, caught in the headlights of my own car. Crazy, isn't it? The car was a write-off, half its original width, but the headlights still lit a path."

I bowed my head, counted bits of gravel around my shoes to fight off the panic.

"Apparently I'd got about a hundred yards. The doctors said I wouldn't have been able to talk, what with my brain bruised and my jaw so badly busted. I would have died if she hadn't found me."

"She?"

"Some librarian from Montreal. Coming to see her kids at Queen's. Taking the scenic route."

"Have you ever talked to her?"

"They say she came to see me at the hospital, but I was so doped up I didn't recognize her."

"What about afterwards?"

Geoff shook his head. "Couldn't do it. Sounds ungrateful, I know, but..."

"And do you come out here often?"

"This is the first time. I thought you'd make it easier."

"Jesus. That was six, seven years ago."

"Yeah."

"Holy shit," I said. "So why me?"

"You were good with Hagar. Calm, you know? I thought I might freak out. But actually, it's not too bad. And I don't remember any of it. You think you should have perfect recall of the moments that change your life; all I have is a scar only wackos can see. What do you figure that means?"

I shook my head and looked at him apprehensively. "Who knows?"

"Thanks for coming, Ian."

"Hey...no problem." I caught his eye. "You want to stick around a while?"

"What, look for bits of my hair? No thanks. I just needed to be able to drive this road again. I was beginning to feel like a prisoner."

Another driver pushed on the horn and accelerated into the corner. We crunched back to the car. Geoff stared at his reflection in the rear-view mirror for nearly half a minute, turning his head slightly right and left, up and down.

He agreed to stay at the house for dinner. Afterwards we sat on the front porch and stared out over the river. Geoff wanted to know if it was serious with Anne. "I don't see you any more," he said. "I figured you either hated me or you were getting married. You seem pretty distracted in class. Still a good teacher, but..."

"I thought you hated my teaching. You said I was too serious, self-important."

"I never said that."

I told him I wasn't sure about Anne, that I couldn't see a future in it. Which was true. When I ran scenarios through my head they involved more of our differences than our similarities. But I liked her a lot. She made me feel truly comfortable, which was more than I could say for anyone else. Every day I felt strangely unsettled as soon as I woke up, anxious. Anne calmed me. I figured I had a choice: leave Kingston at the end of the next school year or marry Anne. I laughed. "If she'll have me, that is."

Then I confessed that I wanted to get back to England. "I'll turn thirty this year. Hell, I left when I was fifteen. I need to visit people before they all die."

"Then go."

"Money. Don't have it. You've seen my fridge. It's been sardines and pasta for weeks now."

We walked into the city. Geoff lived on the main street now, Princess, above the Baskin Robbins. We waited in line for a waffle cone and Geoff pointed at the white ceiling.

"I have circles marked on my floor under the carpet," he said. "Each one of them corresponds to a tub of ice cream. So far I have screwed someone over 26 flavours. I'm saving the Rocky Road for last."

He was joking. He had to be; he hadn't lived there nearly long enough. But upstairs, when Geoff went to the bathroom, I lifted the edge of his old Wilton rug, knowing it was ludicrous but needing to check. Geoff wouldn't have minded if I believed him, that was the problem. It would have been a myth he could live with, I think. The ice cream man.

Geoff offered to lend me the money for a plane ticket, and after a weekend of debating the ethics of it all, I said, "Sure, that's an amazing thing for you to do." Geoff smiled, nodded at me, looked at his shoes. I had the sense, right then, that I was making a mistake, indebting myself to someone who might take advantage.

Anne told me I was stupid to worry. "You've left a mark on him," she said. "Years from now he'll tell stories about you, and they'll all end with how he feels fortunate to have helped you, paid you back for all the inspiration. He'll remember this a lot longer than you will."

"That's what I'm worried about."

Anne scowled.

Two weeks later I was in Oxford again, trying to reconcile memory with the reality of a city that had got along just fine without me. I visited the old high school and all my teachers had either retired or died. The principal — also new — sat me down in her office and told me that Mrs. Harris was out on parole. She had tried to steal jewellery, I remembered, some rings inset with silver sixpences, from a downtown store one Saturday. When the clerk caught her in the act Mrs. Harris had pulled a silver-headed hammer from her purse and beaten the poor girl to death. Broke her skull in two like it was a walnut, the newspaper claimed. I had seen that hammer. Mrs. Harris had used it in French class to bang tacks into the old stone walls. "She served a life sentence," the principal told me gravely. "You've been gone the same length of time. Strange."

And it was. I wandered contentedly along the river I had fished as a boy, and drank greedily at all the pubs I'd been too young for. But there was a hollowness too. I quickly realized that my return would not cure whatever it was that dragged at me, slowed me down. It might fill in some of the gaps, tamp down a few questions, but, truth be told, Oxford was just another place I'd lived in. I could jazz it up any number of ways but that was the bottom line. There were no revelations to be had. So I played tourist.

When I got back, Anne seemed angry, convinced that I'd wasted a golden opportunity.

"An opportunity for what?"

"I don't know," she said, but it was abundantly clear all she wanted was for me to be happier. To smile more.

Our evening degenerated quickly. By the time I was ready for bed we wanted nothing to do with each other. I remember Anne picking at grit beneath a fingernail with a toothpick she found on the shelf where I keep the glasses. She dug at that nail until I thought she would bleed. It irritated me, as did the way we directed our glances away from each other, became bundles of awkward affectation. I had come back from England and now, apparently, we needed some time apart.

"You don't have to stay," I said. "I mean, that's where tonight's headed, isn't it: you leaving?"

She didn't say anything. Just the thin scraping of wood on nail. I tried another tack, something about this being a shitty welcome, but she cut me off, fixed me with a stare.

"I saw Geoff while you were gone, you know. Not intentionally, but he showed up at The Parrot one night."

"The Parrot?" I raised my eyebrows. It wasn't her scene.

"Oh, fuck off, Ian. Some of us from school went. Midterms are over. You, of course, forgot about those."

"I'm sorry."

"Anyway, whatever. I watched him at the bar, drinking Guinness, putting back three pints in under an hour."

"So?" It didn't seem that extraordinary. I'd done it myself. Hell, Geoff and I had done it together. "Did you talk to him?"

"Yes, I talked to him. I went over when my friends left. He's taller than I thought he was. Standing at the bar, side by side, you really get the measure of a guy."

Anne was agitated. She flicked the toothpick onto the carpet and then nudged it around with a bare foot, as if she was trying to thread the wooden needle right into the fibres of the carpet. I let her work at it, fascinated.

Finally I asked, "What did he have to say for himself?"

"Not much."

I waited again, it was so obvious she wasn't done. She stopped fiddling and looked over. "He tried to pick me up."

I sank into my chair. I still remember the springy give in the cushion, the way it threw me back towards Anne, its tough blue wool.

She recounted how Geoff had started with pleasantries. How when she noticed his boot on the brass footrail, knocking at her shoe, she had ignored it. Then he started holding her look, she said, and it was obvious.

"How far did it go?"

"Far enough. I told him he was an asshole; who did he think he was? And he said something like, 'Hey, come on, I paid a lot of money to get you alone like this.'"

"See! See!" I stabbed at the air.

"I laughed at him. I mean, how corny does it get? Then I told him to piss off."

"Did he?"

"No, he grinned at me like a little boy. I think by then he was drunk. So I just left."

Anne stared at the line where the wall met the ceiling, as if she were under water and that's where the surface was. She stood up. "You want some tea?"

I said, "Scotch, maybe," and we both giggled. It was ridiculous, but the story seemed to have eased the tension. I suppose Anne must have been frantic, wondering if I would hold her responsible, ask her what she was wearing. Evidently I'd reacted the right way. It made up for how England had affected me. I was suddenly happy. I was thrilled.

I called Geoff's number from my office on campus the next day, but couldn't reach him. Classes were only a couple of weeks away. And then I tried again from a coffee shop I liked to write lesson plans in. It seemed pathetic, the anger that had bloomed in me overnight. I could see the headlines: PROFESSOR HUNTS DOWN STUDENT. When I first met him, I had been jealous of Geoff's exciting life, of how things happened to him. Even the car accident, its mysterious scars, held an odd charm. But now that I was part of that life, its next chapter, I felt too old for the game, decrepit.

I had dinner in front of the TV and talked to my sister in Boston for a while. I told her what had happened and she said in America that sort of betrayal was likely to get a man killed. "You should at least let him know you're truly pissed off."

I sat there nodding at a nearly empty whisky bottle. For two hours I considered my options, tried to decide whether it was possible Geoff had fabricated a friendship with me to get to Anne. That seemed unlikely, even to my overactive imagination. But the notion ate at me. I swilled back the Scotch and threw on a sweater. I stopped in at The Sleeping Bear for another drink. I stared up at a sitcom playing on the dusty big-screen TV. When my drink was done I laboured back up the three steps to street level and made for Geoff's apartment.

After peeking into Baskin Robbins to make sure he wasn't there I went upstairs, then along the filthy linoleum-floored hallway. The smell of curry wafted in, as if hurried by a fan, from 111, sandalwood incense from 112.

I rapped on Geoff's door. All I could smell now was wood. I ran a finger over the door's surface. It was oily; my knuckles and fingertips were yellow.

"Who is it?"

"Geoff, it's me."

He opened the door and I saw I had woken him. He wore a white singlet and some of those pale green surgeon's pants that are never supposed to leave the hospital. His arms really were quite defined now. Geoff was turning into a big man. I strode through the door and pushed it closed behind me. Geoff wiped dramatically at his eyes with a curled babyish fist. It was a sign I wasn't welcome. He turned his back and wandered towards the kitchen. I scanned the room for any sign of a female presence. I felt like a contract killer. I had absolutely no idea what was going to happen next — only that it was something I wouldn't want witnessed.

I stole up behind him and took a breath — had to turn my head sideways, I was so close. When Geoff sensed me there and made to spin around I shoved him. He sprawled forwards and down, crumpling onto the futon's beige cover. When he rolled over all I saw was fear. I thought he might cry.

I pointed at him, pointed hard if that makes any sense, and he brought his legs into his chest. Foetal.

"Leave me alone," he whimpered. "Just leave me alone."

I was shocked. The effeminate display, the unguarded child-ishness of it, sent shockwaves through me. I felt ludicrously drunk, reeling, falling down blotto. I wanted to throw up. Geoff started to cry.

"You shouldn't have done it, Geoff," I said, my voice break-ing. I felt shaken up, dizzy. Geoff could have reacted this way on the street, in a crowded classroom, and I would have been no more embarrassed. I spied a bottle of wine open on top of the fridge and I grabbed it. As I swigged Geoff peered up at me, immobile but for his eyes. Bits of carpet grit stuck to the soles of his bare feet, thin red threads like capillaries. His hair was pushed up behind his head as if static raged through his body.

"There are glasses in the rack," he said and I tipped the bot-tle away from my lips. Bordeaux smashed about inside.

"You want me to use a glass?" I bent over Geoff's body. "You want me to act properly, in a civilized manner? Is that what you thought I did in Oxford, practise the Queen's English and brush up on etiquette?"

It was nonsense. It wasn't what I felt, or what I wanted to say. I sounded like a little girl. And Geoff, I hadn't wanted to reduce him to this. I put the bottle down on the window sill and peered up Princess Street. A young couple in high school jackets clambered out of a cab and entered the movie theatre. Who knows, I thought, they might be students of mine next year. A bearded bedraggled guy in a stained brown corduroy jacket stood on the corner by the book store, his hand out for spare change. He looked like a Classics professor I knew vaguely. But I had seen him earlier in the week. People, I was sure, didn't fall quite so fast.

Geoff used my few seconds at the window to scoot for the bathroom. I turned in time to see him running. From behind the thin locked door he told me he understood why I was pissed off. "But you should go away," he said. "This isn't going to solve anything. This *abuse*."

His whining enraged me. I wanted to smash all his record albums, or pour wine over the futon and carpet. I felt impotent, though, as if I had accomplished nothing. My sister's obtuse suggestion — that I should kill him — flashed through my head and I laughed, a sad, ugly chortle in a half-empty student's bedsitter. A student. I must be crazy. I rubbed at my forehead, felt the creases in it, and became aware again of the oil on my fingertips. When I walked out I left the door ajar. As if I might return, I guess. So that Geoff couldn't feel secure when he emerged from the bathroom.

I never told Anne what I had done and I don't know if Geoff ever contacted her. For a few weeks I expected a call from the dean's office, a letter saying an official complaint had been filed and my contract would not, in the end, be renewed. But nothing ever happened. It was half-way through October before I saw him again, and then only from a distance. He was hurrying across the rugby field, presumably from one class to another, a load of books under one arm, a pretty Chinese girl skipping happily alongside him. And it was increasingly rare that I thought of him. His presence was no longer threatening, or angering, or even saddening. He was a dim figure, a set of memories, a few synaptic pathways I slowly cultivated for other, more academic matters. The year after that, he was gone.

Anne showed me the newspaper this morning. She had finished feeding the baby and was relaxing when she came across the article. Geoff, we discovered, had moved out to Vancouver Island to work in a marine research facility. In a freak accident yesterday he fell overboard and drowned as he and two colleagues tried to tag a whale. "There were no nets to get caught in," the spokesman for the centre said, "or we would have hauled him back up. Geoff was a wonderful colleague and a dedicated scientist."

I put the newspaper down on the table. "How did you even find this?" I said. It was a small article. There was no picture.

Anne stared blankly.

I re-read the headline: MARINE RESEARCHER DIES IN WHALE TRACKING ACCIDENT. "I don't get it."

"Isn't that just so Geoff," Anne said, shaking her head as if it was all so obvious.

"Is it?" I was mystified. I didn't see the connection. I wanted to push a little but Anne's beaming, desperate smile turned suddenly to tears and she buried her face in her hands. I re-read the piece. It didn't sound like the Geoff I knew. The field of work was right, biology, I just didn't see him as the seafaring type, the committed environmentalist. Anne, though, was howling. I didn't know what to feel. No idea.

At supper I thought about bringing it up again but Anne was still too fragile. Give it a few days, I thought. He's dead, after all. But later, when she went to bed, I came into the study and started to put some of it down on paper. I thought it might help explain things. And now I can see by the little mahogany wall clock Anne bought for my birthday that it's almost 4 a.m.; I should get some sleep, try again in the morning.

Brush-Off

When Martin woke on Saturday the dog was missing. He had a throbbing, lager-induced headache, as well as the vague sense that someone had been trying to contact him during the night. He checked the answering machine but there were no messages. He still believed that Sarah would eventually call. But who knows? After all, she'd been gone eleven days. He'd been drinking too much and let the house fall apart, something he was all too aware of as he hunted the dog, opening closet doors and poking his head in, calling the beast every filthy name he could think of.

The phone actually rang about noon. Ten debilitating minutes later, when he placed the buzzing receiver carefully, respectfully, onto its cradle, Martin wanted to drop to his knees and thank the gods at Bell Canada for their unswerving dedication to improvements in telecommunications technology. He leafed through the directory, found the right four number combination: 1-1-6-9. He dialled and waited. Then a voice: *We're sorry, the number cannot be reached by this method. Please hang up now.* Damn! Sarah had blocked the call. She was on to him, or else she was getting advice from someone. Martin imagined Sarah's shrewish kleptomaniac friend Lisa prodding, "He'll trace the call, you know he will. But you can stop him from doing that. Look, here, I'll show you."

Stupidly, he had picked up expecting it to be the library checking on an overdue book, or Video Hut saying, *When are you returning the Charlie Sheen flick? It's been reserved and you're already a day late.*

So he was surly. "Hello," he barked, tucking the receiver under his chin while he ran a finger through last night's hockey scores.

"Martin?"

"Yes."

"It's Sarah."

"I know." He sat upright, stared vigorously into the room. "You okay?"

"I came by for the dog."

"So I see." He smacked himself in the forehead.

"You said I could."

"Where are you, Sarah?" There was no answer and Martin tried to discern hints of her environment in the background. A train whistle, ocean waves, that sort of thing. He had seen it work in the movies: *Blowout, The Conversation.* He needed a good tape recorder, a way of replaying and analyzing noise; an instrument much more sensitive than his ear. But it was hopeless, as if Sarah had called from a padded room.

"I don't think it's a good idea for me to tell you that."

"Why? You think I'll come banging on the door middle of the night, wake up all Lisa's neighbours? I'm not bothering you at work, am I?"

"Believe me, that's the one and only thing I'm grateful to you for. But it's not Lisa, so don't waste your time."

He tried for a simple "Okay," but it emerged weak, submissive. He was a wreck. He wanted to run a list of other names by her, but backed away from the idea. Why was it so damned important to know where Sarah ate dinner, where she slept?

"I took the car as well," she said. "I guess you noticed by now." She paused, took a loud breath that seemed to suck all the air from around him. Martin moved as far as the phone cord would allow, craned his neck to see out the window. The paved driveway stretched black and spacious. "And I know you're going to say it's ours. But Martin, I need that car to get to work. If you get a job interview out of town or something, maybe I can drop it off. Or you could rent one. Hell, ours is a heap of junk anyway. It wouldn't hurt to show up in something that's not falling apart. And I'm sorry to have come in the middle of the night, but I really think we've done enough talking. Any more and we'll start throwing stuff."

The rush of words was intended to shut him up. It was a favourite tactic whenever Sarah felt uncomfortable, and the recognition made Martin want to grin foolishly, or embrace her, burst into tears. He said, "If this becomes permanent, we'll have to sell it. I'll need the cash."

"You'll find work, I'm sure you will," Sarah said. "It's not worth much money anyhow. You could never certify it again."

"Hey, even if it brought $500."

She bristled. "Are you saying that you want 250 bucks from me?"

Martin blushed, leaned low over the kitchen table. The sour smell of old olive oil and dish detergent oozed from the wood. He wanted Sarah to know it wasn't about money, not at all. But he had been through the bank book and soon he would need every penny he could get his hands on. "That's not it. Honest."

"*Honest!* Martin, come on. You must know how ludicrous that word sounds in your mouth."

He shrugged in the empty room, sensed Sarah gathering herself, mustering what strength she had left. "We shouldn't do this to each other," he said, but at the same time he tried again to visualize the room she sat in, willing to believe in all sorts of psychic phenomena. The emotions here were strong, electric, and it stood to reason they would be more informative. "How is work?" he asked.

"Fine."

"Do they know what's going on?"

"Why do you ask?"

It pained him how easily suspicion flowed through Sarah. But hers was a reasonable question, and besides, he didn't trust his motives any more either. "I don't want your every waking moment to become a torture for you, that's all," he said.

"Then don't go broadcasting why we've broken up, not the details anyway. That story is humiliating for me, Martin. It won't matter how humbly you deliver it, or how much you try to shoulder the blame for what happened — and God knows you had better do that much! — people are going to walk away making ghastly little movies in their head. They're going to imagine the two of you hunched over the couch like shaved dogs. They'll laugh. They'll get points for telling the story at the pub. We'll be ridiculed, Martin. And I don't want people pitying me. You understand? Can you keep that ego of yours in check enough to realize that this story doesn't flatter you?"

"I've told you I'm not proud of it, Sarah."

"Yeah, okay. Just tell me you're not announcing it to the world."

"I'm not." He picked absent-mindedly at a soft apple in the fruit bowl, rolled it back and forth across the table, loosening the dark skin over the flesh. He sensed the gulf between them widening. "So, what are you telling people?"

"Nothing if I don't have to. And if I feel I have to say more, I tell them that you're having an affair."

"The affair's over, Sarah. *Affair* isn't even the right word. I..."

She stopped him. "Martin? Listen to me." He pictured her putting her hand up, playing traffic cop. He wanted to ask if she still wore her wedding ring, or if it had been replaced by a slim band of untanned skin. But it seemed so intimate, so far beyond the scope of what was appropriate. "I don't care any more if it *was* an affair," she said. "Or how many times it happened. The frequency isn't what's important here. Get it?"

He nodded. He needed desperately to hear music, something loud enough to drown out the thunderous racket behind his eyes. "Fair enough," he told her. "But can I at least call you? Check in, make sure you're okay?"

"No, you can't. I'll call you if there's anything to say. There are a few bits and pieces I want from the house, but those can wait until I get my own place."

"You left the book you were reading."

"I'll start something else. I really just wanted you to know the dog was okay." She stifled a giggle. "And that the car hadn't been stolen, of course. You must have been pretty surprised." She laughed again, more sadly. *Our last shared joke*, Martin thought despairingly. And: *Pay attention, this is the last happy moment.*

"I've got to go," she said. "I have a meeting scheduled."

"Okay." He came close to blurting that he was sorry, would she forgive him, but it was too late.

"Bye," she said.

"You bet."

After she was gone he listened for a while to the electric hum in the phone line. And then, when he discovered that he couldn't trace her call, he went for the stereo, loaded a CD with indecipherable lyrics and a pounding bass line. A dull brass candlestick on the speaker shuffled forwards like a reluctant high diver and then fell to the carpet. Its six-inch mauve candle snapped, but the two sections were held together by the wick, a glistening thread like the ligament in a piece of chicken.

That night he started awake, remembering Sarah never worked on weekends; she said the company didn't pay enough to warrant that sort of dedication. It meant she'd lied about having a meeting. He found it impossible to believe that she could deceive him so casually, so carelessly. It didn't matter any more where Sarah was living. She was gone for good. A white panic snaked within him. He burrowed deep under the blankets, suddenly tortured by the persistent tick of a bedside radiator, the animal roar of a roadsweeper chugging along outside. Gingerly, he reached one bare arm over the edge of the bed, timid as a feverish child, and felt for the rum.

Moth

By ten in the morning Green was on his way home from the
station. He had stayed as long as he could, poring over old
weather charts in the staff lounge, trying to calculate the limits
of a hurricane's influence. But he knew there was no way of
telling. Green was approaching the conclusion, slowly, deliber-
ately, that there was no weather system, no event in the world,
too small to be important. Green had read of the butterfly beat-
ing its wings in the Amazon, about chaos theory, fractals. He'd
thought about the interconnectedness of everything. It made
sense to him, it worked. But it made his job impossible. He was
paid a small salary to reduce the earth's climatic complexity to
a simple schematic, a three-day forecast.

The Grim Weatherman they called him. Not just at the TV
station, behind his back, but in the coffee shops, the drug
stores, behind the counter at the library. Green suspected
Leslie, the station's new copy writer, of inventing the moniker.
Green had seen her sitting in the European Deli, shushing her
friends when he came in, tapping forearms, clearing her throat.
Yeah, he was pretty sure it was her, Hurricane Leslie, churning
up the sea around the island that was Green. Bottom line here:
his mood was justified. Because you couldn't predict the weath-
er. And if there were too many variables to make those two

floodlit minutes of prognostication more than a nightly stab in the dark, it was all for nought. It was grim, and grim, Green thought, was where the weather was headed.

He turned north on Gardiners, falling in line with a stream of focused, lonely people in their empty MPV's, their Many People Vehicles. These women, Green mused, would affect the weather too. If you got enough of them needing toothpaste, running out of toilet paper. Hell, if you locked them all indoors with enough supplies for three years, that would change things. It was hopeless. Everything. He leaned on the horn at an old man peering desperately over the steering wheel of his Explorer. The senior navigated the left-hand turn at Princess as if the road bordered an abyss, as if across the white line lay certain death. Green whipped around the outside, gave him the finger and pulled furiously into the mall parking lot.

At the station they thought his worked-up state had to do with his mother, her illness, Green knew that. The worried *how is she's? the anything we can do's?* the way Al Joseph, his boss, let it go when Green snapped at someone. But that was okay. It gave Green some breathing room, distracted everyone from the real problem — the futility of prediction. Still Green knew that even a page one headline declaring meteorologists fools and wilful deceivers wouldn't jeopardize his position. People still read horoscopes, right? And weather forecasting was better than that. There were elements of truth, strands of logical reasoning, parameters within which you could take what he had to say seriously. You just had to know the limits. Mostly, though, this line of thought didn't work anymore and Green simply offered the forecast in a monotone, trying not to look right into the camera. It was a risky thing, this personal integrity business. If he kept it up, grim would become unbearable, unemployable.

Green waited for the pimply boy in the drugstore to overcome the obvious humiliation of his uniform and pull back the long glass wall, let the first customers in. He headed for the one aisle he knew, the one with the chalky milkshakes his mother survived on. He grabbed a six-pack of the strawberry, the same in chocolate. Green assumed they were labelled that way, with a pretence at variety, to make the caregiver feel better. His mother said they all tasted exactly the same: *not too too bad*. He picked straws that had a one-inch accordion section near the top so they could be bent to any angle. His mother liked them. *They seem less childish, more adult*, she said, and he didn't have the heart to laugh at her.

It was cancer. In the stomach, the colon, the liver, the blood. They said it had started in the lymph nodes. The blood was the courier, dropping off diseased molecules at every address like junk mail. She was still taking chemo — the doctors insisted — but Green knew no one expected it to work. All Agnes did now was watch television in the sunroom at the back of the house. Green led her in there at six every morning, and when he got home again, around eleven, he put on *The Price Is Right*. She used to do it herself, but now she was too weak to even work the remote. When Green returned to the station at four she was ready for *Oprah*. Or she was dozing, or throwing up in a pale blue bucket he'd bought at Wal-Mart. It was hard to predict. Green had tried, but again, the big picture, the grand scheme, eluded him. Once he had become frustrated with her inactivity, wondering if she was faking it, even a little, and he left her bucket in the kitchen, thinking it wouldn't kill her to get it herself. He'd found her lying in her own vomit in the doorway. She had tried to make it, she weeped, really. Green yelled, called her names, and then locked himself in his bedroom and cried.

When he manoeuvred the brown Dodge into the driveway, the dog next door started up. This mongrel was keeping his mother awake, depriving her of peace just when it seemed cruellest. Green put down the cans in their white plastic bag, the flimsy handle stretched to its stringy translucent limit, and leaned over the fence. The dog, part husky, part Doberman, strained at its metal chain, front legs pawing desperately for traction, digging a little trench. Spit plumed, the rubbery black lips rolled back like an awning, shark teeth slashing the air. Green's heart leapt a little; he gripped the arrowpoint tops of the fence. It's a cartoon dog, he thought, not for the first time. An adult cartoon. Piece of shit, he thought. Mongrel cur.

He had tried talking to the owners.

"We see you on the news," he'd been told. "You don't seem as happy as you used to. Not that you were ever exactly... enthusiastic."

"It's your dog, I'm afraid, Mrs. Puddle," Green had said seriously. "It's changing my outlook."

"Oh, I can't believe that. She's just being protective."

Green snorted. "Protective! Of the plywood kennel your husband threw together, I suppose. Of the five shit-crusted yards of dirt it lives in."

"Home is different things to different people," Mrs. Puddle had said, casting one eye out over the wasteland her yard had become.

Green sensed, for a fleeting second, an ally. He put his hands on his hips, took in the gathering cloud cover. "My mother's very sick. She doesn't need the noise. I'm worried what all the commotion is doing to her."

"I would worry about yourself, I think," Mrs. Puddle said gravely. "You seem tired on the air. Is that what you call it still: *on the air?* Or is that just for the lay person like me? I suppose you say something more technical, do you?" In the background the dog yelped, tried to break its own neck by hurling itself beyond the chain's full extension. Green gave up, but made a mental note to talk to his mother, ask her how often she was bothered by the dog. "Lovely talking to you, Mrs. Puddle," he said. "Glad we could see eye to eye on this matter. Thanks very, very much."

His mother was asleep on the sunroom couch, Geraldo Rivera scuffled with a couple of young Nazis. Green had seen the footage on the news, months back, and wondered, idiotically, why they would air the episode twice. He stood still, waiting for the fight to end, for Rivera to reach up to his bloodied nose, feel the misaligned cartilage. It saddened Green to think his mother had to suffer this dreck every day, to see the psychic malaise of a continent informing her physical frailty. The world was full of superstition and hatred. Green smiled grimly in the thin-walled room, heard the chain outside being pulled over the ground, saw the dog peering through the fence. He pulled the crocheted blanket up to his mother's chin and poked at the volume control. He picked up the scattered newspaper, then felt her forehead for warmth, some sign that blood, however venomous, still coursed through her body.

These days the refrigerator was always full of leftovers. Shepherd's pie, soup, plain yoghurt, pieces of fruit shrivelling in the crisper. It was hard to eat heartily while someone you loved sucked windily at a translucent straw, the liquid rarely climbing more than half-way to her mouth — as if gravity in her world was more potent than in his, was pulling her earthward, to its source, taking her under. It pained him to have to tip the gaudy can so the straw would transport pink froth her way like industrial effluent. Agnes had wheezed, "You're showing sympathy pains, Green. As I lose weight so do you. You've got to snap out of it, son. I want it to be you that carries me out of this house, not a black-suited stranger. Gives me the creeps, the thought of that."

He ate a banana and checked in on her again. Her body had shifted. One bony arm was bent over her head, a loose-skinned leg flopped over the edge of the day-bed, escaping the blanket. In a healthy woman it might have been erotic. Out the picture window greyer skies and the mad dog ranging beyond the strobe of fence like scudding cloud, digging, digging. Green slid open the door to let some air in, and the dog heard him, sounded the alarm. Green pulled the glass across again, sealed them in.

He put laundry on, moving a hamper full of paisley bandannas, stretched-out underwear, and nightgowns pricked at the elbows with blood and dotted all over with pukey bits, into the washing machine. The water flooded in and the drum heaved its load around, threw it out from the centre.

He went upstairs and dialled Sylvia's number. It was supposed to be over between them. But she was at home, he knew. Whatever else she had planned for the morning, Sylvia always had lunch with her kids. They sprinted from school as if Mother Theresa awaited them. Green hated kids, he had told her so at the bus stop after a movie. "I don't understand what's going through their heads. They look at you, and it scares me. It's stupid, I know, but I can't get over it. Your kids make me feel like I'm at an eternal job interview."

"My kids do this to you, or all kids?"

"All kids. Nothing personal, Sylvia, I'm just no good with them."

"You said, 'My kids'."

"I'm sorry."

"Don't you remember being a kid, Green? Adults intimidated you. There is no kiddie conspiracy. They're not planning to expose you."

There was no convincing him. Green had felt himself backing away physically, edging from the bus stop, over the sidewalk, until his back was against the wall of the bank building. Behind Sylvia he could see the hospital, its mirrored front, the cancer ward windows embedded anonymously in it.

"Then it's no good," Sylvia said decisively.

"What?"

"Us."

"You're kidding."

Sylvia said no, she needed someone who'd grown up, someone who could take on the responsibility of kids. She didn't have time to screw around with a little boy. "You're what, Green, thirty-seven? And you live with your mother."

"She's sick," Green snapped.

"She's dying. But if she wasn't you'd still be there, Green. You've been there as long as I've known you. Sometimes I think all your stories of a married life, a divorce, are just that. Stories." She paused, tipped her head back and bit her lip, appeared to study the bank's sign, its blood-red rectangle. "It's just no damn good, Green." She had turned and made to accelerate away. To Green it seemed as if she moved supernaturally, as if she had been pulling for months against an elastic band, a bungee cord, and the effort had suddenly proved too much, she was giving in to forces that would take her from him. He was infuriated. He grabbed at her, violently, persuaded that he understood what was happening, and she shrieked.

"Let go of me."

He held tighter.

"Green!"

He still couldn't release her. Sylvia slapped at him with her free arm and he dug in his nails. Didn't know why. Sylvia winced and when he saw that he let go. The way her flesh had given under the pressure, and the certainty that he had left marks, intoxicated him. The world swam. He put his hands out behind him and leaned against the rough brickwork, shackled by his own weight. By the time his focus cleared Sylvia had scurried half-way across the street. Two old women in similar beige raincoats muttered something about him and clung to Zellers bags; they turned their backs when they saw him watching. A girl in a brown polyester blouse poked her head out of the donut store, scanned the street and then disappeared.

Sylvia finally picked up the phone. "Hey there, stranger," Green said, pushing his head back into the green tartan armchair. Even now, alone, an embarrassed smile contorted his face. There was no response. "It's me."

"Leave me alone, Green." It sounded resigned, firm, uninterested in what he had to say. Or in an apology.

He tried anyway. "Sylvia, I'm..." He searched for the right words, but before he found them Sylvia hung up. Green listened intently to the bland hum, as if convinced voices were hidden within it. He remembered reading that in the old days you could hear wind in the phone lines, tell what weather was coming your way. But this tone was flat, all nuance drained out of it by new technologies. Technology was the answer to everything, he supposed, an answer and a curse. Green whistled.

Shit. Goddamn. It added up to nothing, this chaos of half-baked notions. His head was a mess.

It was middle of the afternoon before Agnes woke up. She slept more now and Green didn't know if it was the cancer, the chemotherapy, or both. Maybe she wanted nothing to do with this world anymore. Green did what he was told. He turned up the television and found *The Young And The Restless*. "Jack is up to something," Agnes whispered, hoarse. "I know he is." She wanted to sit up. Green had considered his mother indomitable for so long. He thought he got his strength from her, but now, watching her struggle, sensing that she had given in to the cancer, he would have to rethink that notion. Or give in himself.

"I could rent movies for you. Some classics," he offered, and noticed how the light bathed her and made her look like a colourized black and white movie. It caused him to talk slowly.

She shook her head. "They end too soon. Or they go on too long. Everything in the movies gets wrapped up so neatly."

"Earlier it looked like you were dreaming," Green said, getting down on his hands and knees in front of her, pulling wrinkles out of the duvet, feeling a need to fuss, to mother. "Do you remember?"

Agnes stared into the room's air, started to shake with the effort to recall something. "Bits," she muttered.

"Tell me," Green said, anxiously, hoping that insight and clarity, significance, might drain from her as readily as life.

"It doesn't have a plot."

"That's okay," he urged.

"It's nothing, really."

"Go on, anyway."

"It's no good, Green. Damn it, just leave it alone." She kicked feebly with her feet, a toddler's tantrum, and a pink slipper dropped to the carpet. "I've done all I can for you."

He brought her one of the milkshakes, strawberry, held out the bendy straw. "We'll have to hook up your chemo afterwards. It's Tuesday."

Agnes sagged. "How many is this?"

"This is it, the last one. You go back in next week."

She sucked, her cheeks hollowing, as if the meat had been scooped from the bone's frame with a melon baller. Green gave her twenty minutes and then wheeled in the IV unit, with its squeaky rubber wheels, its waist-high beige handgrip. He left again and fiddled next to the sink with the needle, the plastic pouch full of poison. Like a bag of milk, he thought. Milk, for Christ's sake.

When Green padded across the carpet, Agnes jerked her head towards the window. "You hear that dog?" And Green did hear it, realized that it was always there, a part of the universe's background noise. Radiation. "The way it goes on makes me laugh," Agnes said. "So angry all the time. Sad to be like that all the time. Don't you think?"

"I think they should show more respect for you, is what I think."

"Oh, Green. They're not doing it to get at me."

"I didn't say that."

"It's a dog, Green. We don't have any control over dogs. Not really. We chain them up."

Green waited for her to go on but she didn't and he pulled the yellow latex hose tight around her arm. He tapped at her yellow skin, coaxing the blood vessel up. When it rose to the surface, finally, a soaked black log, he slipped in the needle, grim with the professionalism of it all. Agnes closed her eyes. The muscles in her face contracted, a little pained breath hissed into her.

Green stopped, logic suddenly evasive, fuzzy. "We can wait. Do it tomorrow. You might be stronger."

Agnes didn't open her eyes, didn't do anything.

Green waited, then retrieved the needle, pulled it from her like a long grey sliver, silver birch, ash. It was ridiculous, he thought, to inflict this on her, but thinking also that if she objected, signalled in any way, he could start again. He pushed a wad of cotton wool against her arm, staining it red. Agnes' eyes were screwed shut. Defiant, Green thought. Or afraid.

He slipped away and boiled the kettle, heady with what they'd done. He mixed the bubbling water with two crumbled Oxo cubes — beef — and added the chemotherapy drugs. He hid in the kitchen knowing they had to stay away from each other. He waited for the mixture to cool, watching the steam twist into the room. He tried to follow each strand as long as possible, past the point where it disappeared. There was a pattern in the way it rose on the convection currents. All he had to do was extrapolate correctly from what he could see and he would be able to plot the course of the invisible. Water becomes air. Man becomes transcendent. When the steam was gone he changed into his work clothes. And when Oprah appeared on the sunroom screen he kissed Agnes quickly on the forehead and darted out the side door with the chemical soup, saying, "Get some rest." He carried the broth, slopping some over the driveway and the foot-wide strip of grass that separated their house from the Puddles'. He called to the dog — "Bruno, Bruno" — and slipped the bowl under the fence. Bruno swaggered over, sniffed suspiciously, and then began slurping. Green saw no sign of anyone in the Puddles' house. He retrieved the bowl, an empty Parkay tub, and tossed it into the garbage can. He drove away whistling. "Whistling! Shit, can you believe it?" he said out the window. He turned up the radio, whistled some more, a tune of his own, nothing to do with the song being played.

Al Joseph commented on his mood. So did Sid Harris, the head newsman, who slapped him on the back, called him "The Happy Guy."

Green got on the phone in the lounge and called Sylvia. When she picked up, he put the receiver down, severed the connection. He called again, three times, four. Watched the clock hands twitch towards six. The room smelled of cigarettes and the stained teak arms on his chair felt greasy. He stared at the TV monitor suspended from the ceiling. Heard his own name in an ad for the suppertime broadcast. He was a celebrity.

A public figure. He pondered how it changed people's lives, carrying his name around in their heads, whether the sound of it triggered a chemical reaction, caused synapses to fire in a particular sequence. The ramifications were enormous. Think about it. He affected the very structure of everyone's brains just by what he did, by his presence. The sound of his name. The clothes he wore. And by the weather forecast he gave. Wild.

Sid Harris pushed through the swing doors in his expensive blue suit, polished brogues, silk tie. He was thin-limbed, lanky without a desk in front of him. You couldn't do the weather with a body like that. He plopped himself on the couch; his feet left the floor as he folded. "Sylvia just called," he said, looking sheepishly at his hands, his immaculate nails.

Green's pulse picked up. "And?"

"She said to tell you not to call her any more. You're scaring the kids. It sounded like she was a bit shaken up too."

"I haven't called her."

"Green! Come on! Four or five times in the last twenty minutes, she says. All from the station here. What's the game?"

Green told him how Sylvia had caused a scene at the bus stop. "I was just trying to calm her down, he said. Next thing you know..." He held his arms up. Sid shrugged, glanced at the clock, then checked his watch. Tapped the dial.

"She screamed," Green said. "Like I was attacking her."

"Wow." Sid arched his eyebrows, shifted uncomfortably. He played with the knot in his tie, wiggling it back and forth. Green saw the politician in his co-worker, the diplomat. You didn't become top guy at the station without knowing how to stay out of trouble. Green considered the massive effect Sid Harris had on lives. Hell, it was like putting something in the city's water supply.

"It does sound like you were wronged, Green Man. Really does." Sid pushed a stray hair behind his ear. Wouldn't want to do that on the air, Green thought. A touch too feminine, that was.

"Thanks, Sid. Means a lot." Green got up to leave.

"...And Green?"

Green spun around, twirled on one foot. "Yeah?"

"The phone calls?"

"No problem."

Green stormed towards make-up. He stopped just once, to dial Sylvia's number. "Bitch," he said to her, "damn bitch," and slammed the black receiver onto its cradle. He felt better.

On the drive home he ran through his on-air performance. He'd been good, he thought, being as objective as he could. These days he tried to talk more about probability and less about actual weather, and he prefaced everything with a disclaimer: "Taking into account the fallibility of our weather-tracking systems..." It was clunky, but it made Green feel better. Tonight had told the viewers it was going to rain. "Almost no doubt about it," he'd said. "Take a miracle to head this baby off. No pretty monarch is going to save you from 20 or 30 millimetres tonight, my friends." Rain speckled the windshield. Home run, he thought. Yesireee.

The Dodge's headlights swept the Puddles' home, their yard, the long fence. There was no sound, no attack, when Green slammed the car door and paced lightly up the driveway. But you couldn't read too much into that. Bruno might be making a rare visit to the living room. Or, even less likely, they might have taken the beast for a lope in the park. Green stood on tiptoe at the door, tried to survey the neighbouring patch of desert. Nothing. Then, burning through the darkness, Bruno's eight-foot chain, a glowing pale snake, unmoving.

Agnes, Green supposed, was in bed. He checked the blue bucket and it was clean. He put his hand on the television. Cold. "You okay, Mum? Mum?" The floor vibrated as he bounded over it, down the two steps to the kitchen, across to the stairs. A giant moving through a world of smaller things.

His mother was writing; it looked like a diary. She closed the book, tucked it under a novel. She watched Green, his eyes, while she re-capped the pen. "You leave this alone, Green. Until I'm gone what I think is none of your concern. After that, I don't suppose you'll listen to anything I say."

Green giggled, put a nervous fist in front of his mouth.

"Lovely," Agnes said. "Just what every mother looks for in a son." She laughed and Green waited for it to turn into a cough that would tear like a hurricane through her body. Instead, the chuckle gurgled musically down into nothing and Agnes drew in a breath. Except for one rogue cell somewhere deep inside her, she had been perfect. One lousy cell.

"It was quiet tonight," she whispered. "I was lonely after a while so I came in here. It feels safe."

Green looked around. The room hadn't changed since his father died. Seven years. The mahogany wardrobe still presided over this space, its lead glass mirror better suited to a funhouse. It made Green tall, thin, narrowed him to a point at the waist. "Your hourglass figure," Agnes used to say. "Most women would kill for a body like yours." The curtains were a heavy burgundy velvet that Green swore must harbour dust mites, as well as an odour that was slowly spreading through the whole house. His mother, he noticed, had also begun to smell. The scents battled each other, dust versus decay. Last week he had caught a whiff of both of them, wrestling for dominance in the humid still air of the garden.

"Sit with me," Agnes said, and Green nodded, told her he'd be right back. He poured a stiff whisky for himself and a sliver of one for her. He sat on the edge of the bed, the two of them sipping. He cast furtive glances at the diary, as if at some point it would give up its secrets without him having to touch it.

Green started to talk and Agnes soon dozed. In the pauses in his monologue Green listened for the dog, but didn't hear it all night. In his mind's eye Bruno lay sprawled over the mud like a bearskin rug, legs splayed, eyes wide, tongue lolling. Tiny bits of dirt stuck to the tongue's slick underside, and bubbles of spit had set on the dog's jowls. In each wet sphere Green could see his whole world upside down. He felt momentarily culpable. The wind was picking up and Green hadn't forecast that. He had missed something in the data. Rain smacked against the glass.

"I talked to Sylvia today," he said. "She told me to say hello. I know you don't think much of her, but I really think it might work out for the two of us. We're so similar, you know? Anyway, we talked about going away for a weekend. I'd probably have to pay for it, and we didn't get into that, but it might be good, who knows? I'd like to help her out. We wouldn't go too far, just up to the lake, maybe. And the kids would stay in town — Sylvia says she could get a sitter. I think that's a great idea. What do you think? You think you could find it in your heart to give her a chance?"

Green swirled the last of the whisky and threw it back. Agnes's mouth was open. Green pried her fingers away from her glass. They were rigid. She twitched, dreaming again, and Green emptied her drink. He put his feet up on the bed. Listened.

Lemming Meringue

I was pretty sure Alice wouldn't miss me. So when Jerry asked I said, *Sure, a beer sounds good.* We walked up the street together. The sun strobed behind clouds, made a disco of the world.

Jerry squinted. "Looks like rain blowing in."

I thought he was an idiot. A man could go blind staring at the sun.

In The Parrot a pretty Chinese girl in a bright blue bodysuit had the pool table to herself. Two fat men in lumber jackets tossed darts at a pair of battered dartboards. Three boys skipping school skulked in a corner. They were sharing two pints and one of them must have felt like a third wheel.

The bartender pushed a stream of glasses into the dishwasher. His white shirt was wrinkled and already stained with ketchup. I ordered an Ex and Jerry nodded. "Make that two."

Jerry swung around to watch the Chinese girl. He rested his elbows on the bar and that made him look like a chicken. When the bartender wanted six bucks Jerry acted distracted, so I started a tab. Jerry pointed out that the girl wiggled her backside before every shot. It was nothing conscious, just a routine she'd got into. Like a golfer working into the sand before a bunker shot. When she sank the eight ball there was a smattering of applause and she smirked, then strutted off to the bathroom.

"Coke," Jerry said.

I looked over at him.

"I bet she's in there doing lines right now." He sounded enthusiastic.

I shrugged. "Could be." And wondered idly whether Alice was watching the clock on the kitchen wall yet, pulling back the curtain to check for me.

Jerry claimed to be fresh from Timmins. He told a good story but Alice had hated him from the start. "He's a liar," she'd said. "Plain and simple." I swished the possibility around in my brain as if it were a liquid, trying to weigh the odds. I had met him in a laundromat. His red face had poked suddenly around the door of my dryer and he'd mumbled something about static electricity. He seemed harmless and said he didn't know anyone yet.

I had him over to the house one Saturday and we watched the first period of a Leafs game, shared twelve American beer. The next morning Alice complained that he was trouble with a capital T. She was digging around in the toaster for a trapped bagel and she talked facing the wall. "He's a loser. From the minute he came in I could tell."

I stared at her back. "How?" I could see black panties through her nightgown. "It's just until he gets his legs, Alice. I feel sorry for the guy."

"He was flirting with me. Every time you left the room he'd give me a look."

"I didn't know I'd ever left you alone."

"Well, you did." Alice turned and pointed the butter knife at me. "Many times."

"And he was putting the moves on you?"

"Yep."

"You sure?"

She nodded.

"What kind of look?"

"You know."

The bagel started to burn against the element and smoke poured from the toaster.

"You didn't unplug it when you started poking around?" I said. "Jesus." I yanked out the cord.

Alice put the knife down. Her face was inches from mine. "Don't bring him here again," she said.

I called Jerry on it the same afternoon, but he said it was a misunderstanding. "I was trying to be friendly," he said. "Make her feel comfortable. You know what shy women are like. They don't know where to look. I was just trying to show her I was no threat. Hell, I didn't mean to give her the wrong impression, Pete. Come on, it's me you're talking to."

His line about shy women didn't sit right on Alice but I let it go. I got home late again that night, staggering drunk, and Alice said it was pretty clear where my priorities were.

Every day for a week we got into it and one night she locked me out. I thought I could embarrass her into opening up for me. I yelled up at our bedroom window and banged on the door but she ignored me. I sat on the front step. A kid swooshed by on his bike, throwing newspapers left and right. His simple life made me angry. I imagined the cool air on his face, the easy strength in his young arms, then got up and started screaming again.

Eventually the cops came, and Alice wouldn't come down for them either. I remember thinking, even in my worked up state, that it took a lot of nerve to ignore the cops like that. I hated her for it, put my head back and called her a couple of names. The cops arrested me. No charges, they just locked me up in a cell with no mattress and a steel toilet, then released me at seven in the morning.

I swore off the bars for a few days after that, figuring Alice wouldn't put up with a quick repeat, and told Jerry he'd have to get by on his own. I didn't feel too bad about it. I'd introduced him to a few people and he was a sociable guy. And anyway, I figured Alice would be happy after a week or two, and then she'd suggest maybe I should go out for a pint.

I hadn't seen Jerry at all. But then today there he was in the doorway of Shoppers Drug Mart, stuffing a prescription envelope into his jacket. It was a moment of weakness on my part, I guess, a small break in the fabric of decency I'd cultivated like a new skin.

The Chinese girl returned from the bathroom and Jerry knocked at me with an elbow. "Here she comes," he said. He was like a dog fixated on a squirrel, his thick pink tongue draped over his teeth. If I'd said anything he would have replied, "There's no law against looking," and laughed at me. "Am I right?" he'd say. "Am I right?"

I wanted to finish my drink and head home. Jerry was here for the long haul, but I could still salvage the day with some flowers from the market.

Off to my right two guys were talking about fruit. "You can't beat a good pear, you know," one of them said. "Most people eat them too soon or too late. No one pays enough attention to their pears; they're labour-intensive if you want to get it right." He took a long calculated sip from his glass. "But my God, you get a Bartlett at the right moment, and wow!"

The man's companion nodded in agreement and said something about perfume bottles being designed to look like pears. The two of them cackled like old women, slapping each other's white forearms. The bartender glanced over, but when I caught his eye he played dumb. These two could be brothers, I thought, locked up most days with their ancient mother in a run-down Victorian rowhouse near the water. They were probably out to buy vitamins for her. Or some food for the cat and a bottle of shooting sherry.

Jerry nudged me again. I felt his breath on my face. "Queers," he said. "Queers and druggies. Ain't it great?"

And it was.

Two hours later I got up to phone Alice.

Jerry snorted. "You'll be back here in five minutes saying you've got to leave," he said.

"Maybe so." I tried to make it sound like that would be fine.

I took a leak first and then stood in front of the mirror. It was illogical, but I was sure Alice would know where I was, even over the phone. She was an FBI laboratory disguised as a woman. And where it would take your average G-man weeks to decipher my whereabouts — replaying the conversation a hundred times, picking out the background detail, the clanking glasses, the distant thump of a dart, the band warming up — Alice would deduce it instantly.

Alice sounded like she'd been expecting this call for days. "I knew it wouldn't be long," she said. "It's your own fault what happens to you, you know?"

I imagined her wandering the kitchen as far as the cord would allow, receiver tucked neatly under her chin. She was picking up dirty dishes and piling them next to the sink. Or watering the spider plant that hung in a copper basket going slowly green over the table. She pulled back the curtain and stared out into the laneway. A grackle bashed a grimy walnut shell against the wall of the house and Alice tapped on the glass to scare it away.

"You don't sound surprised." I told her.

Nothing.

"Well I want you to know I am," I said. "Surprised, I mean." I had that wronged schoolboy look on my face; it was the only way I could get the tone right.

A kid with a purple mohawk shouldered past me. I heard him spit into the urinal.

Alice said she was coming down.

"Maybe I should come home instead," I said.

"No. I need a beer. You've driven me to drink."

I wanted to believe she was smiling, but the image I got of her was suddenly foggy. Strange that her reception should be perfect when mine was clogged intermittently with heavy static.

Jerry had two new beers lined up on the bar. I smiled grimly and shook my head. "Well, at least I know how to get you to buy now," I said.

He threw his arms in the air. "What did I do?" He had the seedy look of a beach vendor.

"What if I'd had to leave?" I said.

"Then I'd drink them both."

"Alice is coming." It sounded moody, resigned, and I didn't want that.

"Drink up then, buddy. The end is nigh." Jerry tapped his bottle against one of the new ones and I picked it up.

"I shouldn't do this," I said. "I should wait for her outside and take her out to dinner."

The purple mohawk weaved through the bar. He hopped up on the low stage and sat at the drum kit.

I turned to the bartender. "This is the type of band they get now?"

He nodded.

"This used to be a blues bar. A rock and roll bar."

"Punk's back," the bartender said. It sounded like an explanation he had to give every day. He slotted a spotty wine glass into a rack over the liqueurs.

"What are they called?"

The barman shrugged and pointed at a distant yellow poster. Jerry and I peered that way, both of us leaning our heads forward, screwing up our eyes. Neither of us could read what it said.

"Too old for this shit," Jerry said.

The guy with the thing for pears leaned over and whispered in my ear. "The Lemming Meringues. They're very good." He smiled sweetly.

"Lemon Meringues?"

"Lemming. The *Lemming* Meringues."

"Thanks," I said. "Funny stuff."

Jerry wanted to know if I had made a date. "Alice really will be steamed."

I told him to fuck off. Gays struck me as a weird bunch but the same went for every architect in the world, every mailman.

I pointed with my bottle at the empty pool table. "You want to give it a go?"

The Chinese girl had moved up near the stage. She smoked *Gitanes* and a rich fog swirled around the looming black speakers. There were extra jackets slung over the spare chairs and I realized she must be with the band. A girlfriend maybe. The singer.

Alice arrived half-way through our second game. I'd won the first pretty easily and then Jerry wanted to play for money.

"You think I'm an idiot, right?" I said. But Jerry looked hurt and so I agreed to five bucks a game. To my surprise I was winning the second game too, and toying with the notion that Jerry just wasn't very good. That would fit with Alice's opinion of him.

I watched her size the place up. She was good in bars, confident, like she'd been practising without me.

The two dart throwers stopped their game and leered at Alice. One of them grabbed at his crotch and they both laughed. They started another game, one where they stood with their backs to the board and threw over their shoulder. The first attempt smacked into the wall, three feet wide of the mark.

"Get you a beer, Alice?" said Jerry. He carried his cue stick the way a shepherd might. The heels on his boots were well-worn and he walked so you thought he might, at any moment, tip over backwards.

Alice muttered something. I assumed it was *No thanks,* because she bought herself a Lamb's and carried it over.

I kissed her on the cheek, squeezed her arm.

"Careful, Peter," she said.

I looked at her puzzled.

"Who's winning?" she said.

"Peter is," Jerry said. "Hell of a pool player, that man of yours. Going to take all my money."

I knew he'd brought up the gambling to see if Alice disapproved. But she just rubbed absently at the end of her cue with the chalk. Blue dust misted the back of her hand.

The bartender leaned on the cash register and watched us. I suppose there wasn't much else going on.

"We'll just finish this one up," I said. "Then we can be going."

Another mohawk joined the drummer on stage. This one a bright yellow. Canary, I thought, until Alice said it looked like he had one of those kitchen brooms on his head, and asked if we could take him home with us. She tugged at my sleeve. "Can we?" she whined. She hung her head to one side and pouted.

I grinned. Not because she was funny — she wasn't — but it seemed a sign Alice wasn't too pissed off. Maybe she was glad to get out. And we were together at least, and it was early. And we were pretty much sober.

"We won't be here all day," I told her. "I promise."

Jerry turned silent, focused. I realized he thought Alice would be a distraction for me, a chance for him to get back into the game. But I felt confident, as if there could be TV cameras watching me play and I wouldn't embarrass myself. When he was down to his last two balls I closed it out.

"Give Alice a game," I said. "And give me the five bucks. I'll get us another round."

I watched them from the bar, how Alice kept the table between them, sliding sideways, back and forth. I felt bad. I didn't know whether Alice's dislike for Jerry was rubbing off on me. I was too impressionable. It was the reason I couldn't read a film review before I saw the movie. I wasn't stupid, just lazy when it came to that sort of opinion.

The purple mohawk slammed casually on the drum kit, a pulse that knocked around my head like a blood clot. I'd had four or five beers and noises worked on me differently. The yellow-haired punk strapped on his guitar but left it unplugged. He closed his eyes and mouthed the words to a slow song. He must have run through a couple of verses before he opened his eyes again. I saw the moment when he realized where he was flash through his bloodstream like a speedboat.

The Chinese girl beamed up at him and I made the connection: he was singing about her, to her. It was a love song. I was impressed with myself. I could read the world as well as I could play pool. I was Kreskin, I was The Amazing Randi. I strained to hear conversations from the street, convinced that I might be able to do it. Words welled up in me from nowhere. Voices other than my own.

"Eleven fifty." The bartender tapped me on the back. He pointed at the drinks. "Eleven fifty."

Jerry called out, "Hey, it's like a fucking jungle in here. Do they have to do that now?" He waved his stick towards the stage. The Chinese girl twisted in her seat, the smile gone. Her leather jacket squeaked against the chair.

The bartender tapped at his watch. "Sound check."

The gay guys debated whether to order more drinks. There were two empty martini glasses in front of them. "It is pretty loud for this early," one said.

"To hell with the noise," the other said. He grinned sloppily and caught the bartender's eye. He pushed the empties to the back of the bar and wiggled a finger over the top.

Alice was winning. "I like this game," she said. "Jerry's a real loser...at pool." She grinned.

I wanted to get the hell out. Right then, before it got ugly. But I also wanted to watch the two of them go at it. The indecision made me dodder. I knew how Alice fought, but I knew jackshit about Jerry. He didn't seem the type to shy away from anything.

"It's that fucking drumming more than anything," he said. "It's driving me crazy."

The bartender was shaking the martinis, a shuffling latin accompaniment to the duo onstage. He seemed to be enjoying himself. Jerry gestured at him but he shrugged cheerfully. I think the barman saw all this noise as a way of getting rid of us, like putting an airport next door to our house. The two gay guys sat watching their drinks mix in that shiny metal canister, two dogs waiting on a bone.

The drummer punched down harder on the skins. Maybe he was in on the game. The girlfriend moved her head in circles as if to work out some stiffness, but she kept her mouth fixed on a straw that dipped into a bright blue liquid, Curacao perhaps, that almost matched her bodysuit. A tributary feeding into the main river.

Alice came up behind me. She leaned over my shoulder.

"Prison," she said softly, pushing the word out of her mouth delicately, like it was a butterfly that flew in while she was sleeping. I felt it flitter and disappear. She opened her mouth again. "He told me."

Jerry was glaring at the drummer. I turned and Alice moved her backside away but left her head where it was, next to mine. I smelt the rum on her breath, its ruining sweetness. She took a couple of steps away and poked me twice in the chest with the cue. I looked down and there were blue marks on my shirt, one for each lung. "And you, my friend," she said, "are history."

It felt sexual somehow, like foreplay, but I knew that was dead wrong. "What do you mean?"

Jerry must have shifted his attention from the band. "Hey, whose shot is it?"

"Yours," Alice told him without looking away from me.

Jerry looked over the table. "Shit. Did you take two in a row?"

Alice snorted sarcastically and Jerry peered moodily down at his options.

I watched the two martinis tumble into their glass bowls like mountain spring water. The beer was making me sluggish. I saw condensation forming on the outside of the fancy glasses. When the bartender put them down his fingerprints were all over them.

"What do you mean?" I said again, keeping my back to Jerry, keeping my voice down.

Alice spun away from me. "You screwed up, Peter. You didn't even last a month away from this shit."

"A month?" I was surprised at the time frame. "It was an accidental meeting."

"Oh?" Alice staggered dramatically backwards. "So you *fell* into this place? A strange force pulled you in when you, poor little innocent you, were on your way to the post office? Or was it that some ex-con loser said, 'Hey let's grab a beer,' and the pity you felt for him was overwhelming?"

Jerry moved to be near us.

The pear lovers were watching. For the second time in half an hour I felt like I was on television. Only it wasn't the sports channel any more.

Jerry said, "It's your shot, Alice."

She flashed him a rude smile that seemed to say fuck off as much as it said thanks. She moved behind the white ball, taking solid angry strides. In a house you would have felt the floor move. When she leaned over the table I realized she didn't have the same grace as the Chinese woman. She adjusted to the right angle as if her back hurt.

"It's not going too well, is it?" Jerry said. He stared at the table like a mathematician trying to work out all the possibilities. "I hope it's not my fault."

I didn't know whether Alice could hear him, it was fifty-fifty. She smacked the six into the side pocket and left herself a clear shot at the four.

"That depends," I said. "Alice says you told her you were in prison."

"So?" He turned and looked at me. It was the indignation of someone mortally offended. But it was the beach vendor again too. I felt like I was swimming upstream.

"Well, were you?"

"What difference does it make?"

"A big one to Alice." I realized I was louder now, and shifting the blame.

"Did I hear my name?" Alice leaned on the table, her fingers tucked under so she rested on her knuckles. You stick some cigarettes in the arm of her T-shirt and you've got a dockwork-er, I thought. I looked for her triceps and found them, long and thin, like chicken tenderloins.

"Pete here thinks you're bothered by my past," Jerry said. He sidled towards Alice.

I didn't like the way this was working out, the way alliances seemed fluid, uncertain. I wasn't sure I could rely on anything. The beer tasted stale and I looked again at the cocktails on the bar. The glasses were sweating. The Martini Boys pretended to be talking to each other. We were too preoccupied to turn on them and they knew that.

The Chinese girl sucked at her straw and peered at the bartender — wondering, I suppose, if he thought we were trouble.

The two mohawked punks were on barstools at the front of the stage pecking at a plate of nachos. They were engrossed in their meal and kept their heads down. Two tropical birds gnawing at cuttlefish.

I checked for the three schoolkids but they had finished their two beers and bolted before someone thought to ask for ID.

"You told Peter you were from Timmins," Alice said.

"I am." Jerry looked pleased at how easy it was, this new game.

"But you told me you came straight from prison." She was trying out a prosecuting attorney routine, devising in her head some trap for Jerry.

"I did," Jerry said. "I wasn't lying."

Alice stood up straight. She batted the cue ball from right to left. "But you're from Timmins?"

"Right. You think people are born in prison?"

"So how come you told me the jail part and not Peter? Was I supposed to be impressed?"

"I thought you could handle it better." Jerry pulled a chair over the floor. He sat with his legs splayed in front of him, his beer resting on his stomach. A smile crept over his face. "I thought Peter here was too soft. A nice guy, but too doughy. I thought he'd go running." He waved his beer in my general direction. "No offence, Pete. I like you, that's why I didn't tell you. None of your fucking business either, is it?" He grinned, his teeth a dull ivory in his mouth, fossils.

"What did you do?" I said, draining my beer. It didn't seem to matter what I tried, my mouth wouldn't stay wet.

"Again," Jerry said, "that's none of your fucking business."

I thought about carrying on, pushing for more information. I was worried, though, that Jerry would say he'd killed a man and Alice would say, *That's not so bad.*

She slammed her empty glass onto the pool table. The bartender, for the first time, moved away from his newspaper.

"It's got nothing to do with your being in jail," Alice said. She was exasperated, a nursery school teacher at quitting time. "It's got nothing to do with you, period. As far as I can tell, you're a garden variety asshole. At best you're a guy with too much time out of the loop to know how to act in civilized company."

"You should keep a lid on her," Jerry said to me, reddening.

Alice waited for me to defend her. I think she thought she was indomitable, that she could run on at the mouth as much as she wanted and something would always save her.

"Hey," I said weakly, "it's a free world."

"Not until recently, for Jerry," Alice said.

She headed for the bar but then stopped half-way, maybe realising things needed some redirection. "It's my so-called husband who really ticks me off, Jerry," she said. "You just don't know any better."

Jerry played with the sentence for a bit, his head tipped to one side as if he could think more clearly that way. Alice sidled up beside the martini drinkers.

"A Lamb's for the lady," I heard someone say.

I hated everyone.

"She's trouble, man" Jerry said.

I nodded. "Sometimes."

"She's put you in danger."

"From you?" I said. I knew that's what he meant but it felt so melodramatic, absurd. I got a fresh vision of him poking his hot little head around the door of my dryer in the laundromat.

"Or anyone in here, man." He waved his arms to include the whole room. "Hey, I learned to be real calm when I was inside. But the band up there, they wear their hearts on their sleeves. You don't want to mess with them."

The two punks were wiping their fingers across their empty plate, licking off cheese grease. They looked about seventeen. One of them waved sarcastically at me. It was a learned response to all the attention he got, and I liked him for it. I didn't see what they had to do with anything.

"We should call it a day," I told Jerry. I put out my hand.

"I'm sorry it turned out this way." I thought about blaming Alice but changed my mind. "Friends?" It felt adolescent. I wanted a martini.

Jerry slapped my hand away. "Sure," he said. "That's probably for the best. Another half-hour and I'd be trying to screw Alice. Right after the Chinese chick turns me down." He grunted and rose to his feet. I wondered if I could take him.

He jammed his cue into the rack and headed for Alice. "Gotta go, darling," he said. He draped himself over her shoulders and kissed her cheek. "You don't mind, do you, Pete?"

"Not if this is the end of it."

"Of course he fucking minds," Alice said. She shrugged Jerry off.

The gay guys chuckled and the bartender appeared with a case of beer over each shoulder. The effort showed on his face and he struggled into a crouch next to the beer fridge door.

Jerry slapped me on the back. "She's all yours, buddy. See you 'round." He leaned in one more time and kissed Alice on the top of the head.

"Shit," Alice said. "Sometimes you really wish you'd worn a hat, you know?"

I said nothing. I figured I was watching the final credits. The action was over, why try for some violent epilogue?

Jerry bent his knees until he was at eye level with the Martini Boys. He raised a hand and waved at them, moving only his fingers. He was a natural at the effeminate gesture. "Bye girls."

The one in the chinos, a frail red-socked man, reached into his glass and retrieved an olive. He swirled it in his mouth, sucking away the vodka and the meat. Jerry grinned his bully's grin. But then the stone flew at him, caught him on the bridge of the nose. It dropped to the carpet, rolled an inch or two. We all looked down. Khaki meat clung to the pit.

Alice howled. She rocked back and forth on her stool and her eyes watered. The bartender leapt to his feet — hoping, I think, that someone would repeat the punchline. The gays smiled politely at each other. The spitter dabbed at his lips with a paper napkin. Alice watched him through misty eyes.

Jerry ran a cuff over his cheek. He pointed a finger. "Faggot," he yelled. He aimed at the other one's head. "Faggot."

The bartender moved into Jerry's view. "Hey, knock it off."

"Knock it off?" Alice sputtered. She grabbed a quick breath and then bent double laughing again. "Did you hear that, Peter? He told him to knock it off."

Jerry pointed at the bartender. "You too. Faggot." He waved his hand in front of everyone like a sparkler. "All of you."

The bartender put his hands on top of the bar, prepared to vault over to our side. Jerry made for the door half-running, like a man late for a bus. The bartender regarded his own profile in the mirror a second, his pumped-up chest, and then went back to filling the fridge.

The band applauded, nodded their approval, and the Chinese girl joined in.

"Way to go, man," the purple one said. The fags held up their martini glasses in a perfectly symmetrical gesture.

I didn't say anything. The last five minutes hadn't been good to me. My head teemed with excuses. I searched for smart throwaway lines that would excuse my inaction, a semantic trick that would make a virtue of it.

"You're a wimp," Alice said quietly. She wore the bored, slightly irritated look of a woman who has been woken by Jehovah's Witnesses. "I don't think I knew that about you. I knew enough, but not that."

I stammered something unintelligible and then stopped.

"You did nothing," she continued. "Your only act of defiance today was when you came in here with that asshole. And that wasn't really defiance anyway, was it? You just couldn't say no to him, even if it meant hurting me."

"That's not true. I didn't think it would do any harm."

"Hey," Alice said, as if the thought thrilled her, "you would have let that creep take a swing at me!"

"We should get out of here," I said. "Go somewhere and talk about this." She shook her head and rattled her glass on the bar.

"Another one of these, please."

I figured it must be getting darker outside by now. Headlights were being switched on, stores closing down.

Alice's decision to drink, and drink alone, meant more than it showed. She had always thought I came to these places too much, but now she believed I came because I was weak.

She ignored me, held the dark glass to her mouth so the ice cubes brushed against her lips, chilled them. I thought of insisting that she leave with me. I also considered having a beer in the hope that more drinks would soften us, make it more likely we could leave together. I even thought about fighting back, but Alice would find that laughable. I ordered a whisky and sat looking into it for a sign, trying to read the spirit like tea leaves.

The Boys drained their drinks. "It's been quite a thrill," they told Alice. She shook hands like they were old friends, family. It seemed absurd, the world spinning the wrong way all of a sudden, messing with my balance.

The place was emptying out, people wanting to put in an appearance at home. The stage was dark. The two fat guys had exhausted themselves at the dart boards and they sat with their backs to the wall like marathon runners in desperate need of fluid.

"Come on," I said.

"Come on what?" Alice snapped.

I shook my head and threw back the whiskey. She wasn't coming with me but I still had to leave. I felt like I'd been framed.

On the way out I passed the Chinese girl. She stopped me and asked if I'd finished with the pool table. I told her we had.

"Good," she said. "I think I'm lucky here. Maybe you and your wife want to play us sometime later?"

"Maybe," I said. She looked so eager, her head bobbing up and down as she asked the question, I didn't have the heart to disappoint her.

I pushed into the bathroom. Someone had smashed the mirror

and the sink was full of glass; the counter was like an ice rink. The cinderblock wall where the mirror had been was grey, unpainted. I felt a breeze coming through the cracks from outside, felt it flutter against my cheek. I stood there for a while, imagining myself in the country, hours — days — from the nearest town. Someone was selling lemonade. Two men were hauling an old sofa out to the curb and they nearly tripped over a blue tricycle. They left white trails on the wet morning lawn. Church bells were ringing and the street was full of people I'd never seen before. They were waving.

Jenny Heads for Underwear

We're supposed to be hung over, taking it easy, the tequila's sting laying us low. But I still agree to venture out for a 10-piece box. Me, I can't stand the Colonel, the barbarous reek gets up my nose, in my hair. A lunchtime encounter leaves me feeling like I've spent a lifetime working in a chip truck. But not Jenny. For her the oil's a lubricant, an orally prescribed dose of Pennzoil. A couple glistening wings and she's right as rain, a Formula One driver on life's hectic track. Jenny Villeneuve, you might say.

So I walk in with the box held before me like a rat in a trap. I'm expecting Jenny to be flaked out on the couch, punching feebly at the remote. But I've got it all wrong. She's actually on a stool in the kitchen, spinning, slowly wrapping herself in black phone cord. I look down the hall to the living room, take in the TV's bright green screen, a flicker of scurrying reds. *Soccer Saturday.* Then I listen to Jenny. "Who is it?" I mouth, assuming it's her mum, or someone we ran into at The Parrot last night. Jenny ignores the question but I suspect nothing until she says, after a long period of listening, "So what you're saying...is that it's possible. Have I got that right?"

And apparently she has, because suddenly she's all grins and her spinning picks up. After a bit she stops, using her foot on the lower chrome rail as a brake. She crosses and uncrosses her legs and scratches at her thigh in a distracted, agitated way that says she can't wait to get off the phone now. "Good, good. Well no, you're right, it's not good if it actually happens. But in a theoretical sense, it is good to know it holds water."

I try again, this time out loud: "Who is it?"

Jenny claps a hand over the receiver. "A med student," she hisses. "Friend of Carol's." She stares at the floor, concentrates on a fresh buzz coming at her ear. "No, that's all I needed," she says. "Yeah, I guess it does sound weird. But hey, we homebodies are allowed to question the world too, right? Exactly. Thanks. Yeah. Bye."

"Well?" I say, waving the box of chicken like bait.

She slaps at my backside, and spins away. "Well nothing. Get your street clothes on, Bucko. We're taking a ride."

She swoops and swipes away the chicken, then attacks the bag like a crow going at roadkill. Watching her eat I realize that if I tried a few of those tight revolutions, or experienced a similar enthusiasm of appetite this morning, I would throw up. Plain and simple.

Less than half an hour later we're mall-bound. No idea why. Jenny urges me to weave through traffic, and bounces in her seat, offering extravagant encouragement: *You can take that wimp*, she says mockingly, leaning into the curve. *Quick, ride the G's, Spaceman.*

It's the same in the parking-lot, and again as she tugs me along the main floor. And it's not that I'm reluctant — although that is part of it — I simply can't keep up. Whatever project Jenny's cooked up has resulted in a flow of chemicals to her brain that create energy, a sense of purpose. I am a man lacking said chemicals. I am bereft. My brain bashes about in dry dock, scuffs against the rough inside of my skull.

In The Bay, Jenny speeds through Home Furnishings, Linens, Sports, Books and CD's. I try to slow her down, point at something titled *Wok Like a Man* but she wants nothing to do with it. "Not for you, for me," I plead.

"No time, no time," she says.

She slows entering Lingerie. I'm hopeful, but also aware that, like a speeding train, Jenny may require a mile or two to come to a complete stop. She puts a contemplative finger to her lips, peers deep into areas full of bras, silk panties stretched across clear acrylic hangers so they seem like immense pinned butterflies. I feel like a naturalist entering a grove where exquisite rare deer are known to graze. Or else a taxidermist arriving at work. Jenny flicks quickly through rack after rack of nylons: midnight black, linen, nude. She selects a pair in nude and is gone again. I catch up at the cash register. She is tapping her foot anxiously, checking around. This is just the first stop, obviously, and not the main reason we hauled our swollen brains out to the mall on a Saturday.

"I'm going to leave you here," I tell her, not really faking the irritation.

"Say again?" Jenny squints at me vaguely. She scrabbles through her wallet.

"I've had enough," I say. "I'll wait in the car."

"Whoa, back up there..." she starts, but I put my hand up like a traffic cop.

"You say *Bucko* again and I won't even wait."

Jenny looks hurt, like the new moniker was a gift I've tossed aside ungratefully.

I try explaining myself: "Come on, love, my head's pounding. You've got some prank in mind, that's fine. But leave me out of it." Because that's definitely what's going on here. Jenny loves this stuff. And me? It feels all wrong today, that's all I can say. Sometimes I'm into it. Other times I'm left cold, or freaked out. The pitbull thing, for instance. She pushed that too far. Could have got nasty; it still might. "This isn't a game, you know," I say to her. "Or if it is, I'm not in the mood to watch."

"Again with the sports," Jenny chides, and I grimace. Jenny catches it, senses she's gained a little ground. "Always the same thing," she complains. "I just feel like I'm in the way most days.

I'm a curtain between you and your precious TSN. It's like I'm stopping you from an ideal existence as a...a jock watcher."

"A jock watcher?" I say, uncomfortable with what seems to be an unpleasant inference.

Jenny shrugs, downcast but brightening again. "I make life sporting for you."

"It's an adventure, I'll give you that much."

Jenny winks.

The cashier, a teenaged girl with red hair, a thousand freckles, raises a skeptical eyebrow. I feel like I'm playing subliminal *Jeopardy*, all life's answers hidden from me, revealed only through intimation, obtuse comment and gesture.

"Come on, we're off," she says brightly, pocketing her change.

"If it's somewhere formal, you're out of luck."

"You'll do," Jenny says, giving me a lascivious once-over. Then she drags me away.

The day is picking up steam. It's busier now, the mall teeming with beleaguered parents, snotty Little League kids and wannabe hoodlums. At the food court it's courting rituals over Slurpees and Manhattan fries. A boy with a plate of chicken balls and chop suey eyes a girl lined up at the frozen yoghurt counter. His lips glow sweet-and-sour, his cheeks puffed out like he's hoarding for winter.

Jenny pulls up abruptly outside Zellers and takes my arm. "Okay, you just tag along." She pulls those new nylons from the bag, puts her fist in each leg and stretches them out. Then she throws out the Bay bag but puts them back in their Hanes envelope.

"Jenny," I say. "For Christ's sake."

She looks at me defiantly, says, "It's just another game — a sport," and zips between the chrome posts meant to keep shopping carts either in or out. I'm reminded of a horse leaving the starting gate. My mind, slow-witted as it is, teems with sports metaphors and baseball stats. All of a sudden I'm ludicrously aware of Joe Carter's prolonged hitting slump and Ken Griffey Jr.'s torrid home-run pace. It feels, I realize, like denial. *Face up to it, man,* I tell myself. *Trouble's coming at you, look it in the eye.*

Jenny heads straight for Underwear. It's a more muted display of lingerie than at The Bay, more pale brown, fleshy contraptions in bigger sizes, more modestly cut. Like going back in time twenty years. The carpet underfoot is more ravaged; teddies hang from only one strap as if held disdainfully between thumb and forefinger, evidence of some late middle-age adultery. Rather than butterflies, the panties here are dull, more mothy.

Jenny begins to limp outrageously. She drags her left leg across the broadloom as though it's made of lead, an anchor on her ambition. Like its been slowing her down for years, like the future looks just as bleak.

I shake my head, dismayed, frightened by whatever Jenny's up to. Truth is, I desperately want to get along with people. It's taken me a long time to acknowledge that fact, for me to metamorphose from angry punk into taxpayer. I'm still not wholly convinced it's the right way for me to go, but Jenny's antagonism sits less and less well with me. It makes me edgy, nervous in the world. I feel over-caffeinated all the time.

Jenny hobbles towards a sales clerk and I hold my breath. The girl's name tag reads Mandy and I say to myself, *Sorry Mandy; for the hell you are about to endure, my deepest apologies.*

"Can I help you?" Mandy says. She reminds me of a cousin — Rebecca — a raven-haired, very thin young woman who got a bit part in a beer commercial couple of years back, and instantly my sympathies are with her rather than Jenny. Mandy tosses aside a lurid pink cardigan (as if to say: *look, you are my first priority, above all material things*), and rubs her hands clean of its fibres. She smiles broadly. This girl, I think, has got the employee handbook memorized, and that strikes me as sad.

"I bought these," Jenny says, tugging out her Hanes and waving them in the air. She holds them bulked in her fist but the better part of a leg flails free and I wonder idly whether that's the covering for her good leg or her bad leg.

Mandy nods. She bites at her lower plum-shaded lip. But she doesn't say anything. She's cagey, I think. She's adding it up.

"And look at me now!" Jenny twirls for her, arms out like wings. I become aware, for the first time, of the muzak, a Sting song diluted so thin it nearly evaporates before I recognize it.

Mandy shakes her head and, I'd wager, thinks to herself: *Here we go. Nutjob. Nutjob in Underwear.*

"How about this, then?" Jenny limps around Mandy, swinging her newly deceased left leg. After one revolution — Mandy revolves too, but on the spot, steadily, like a circus ringmaster — Jenny comes to a halt, fakes a pained, even tortured expression. "The leg," she says in exasperation. "For crying out loud: the leg." She slaps at her presumably useless thigh. "It's numb," she shrieks. "I've got no feeling."

Mandy looks dumbfounded. "And...?"

"It's because of your nylons. I'm ruined," Jenny cries.

I take a tentative half-step forward. "She tried to have Hanes her way and it backfired," I say sheepishly.

Jenny pivots sharply. I feel for her but this is far-fetched stuff, ludicrous even. I mean, where's her receipt? Because surely that's the first question. And Mandy doesn't look the least bit impressed.

"I'm sorry, I don't understand," Mandy says. She leans back and rests her backside on the edge of a counter, grips its lip with both hands. *Take your time*, the pose says, *I'd like to hear this.*

"I've come straight from the hospital," Jenny says, her distress impressive. "It took them nearly seven hours to restore circulation. But it still feels numb. Like it's gone to sleep and won't be revived.

"Like it died in its sleep," Mandy says helpfully.

"Exactly," Jenny says.

Mandy frowns and brings her hands up to her face. "How awful. But then I've always thought that if you've got to go, that's the best way."

"Say again," Jenny says slowly.

"In your sleep," Mandy explains.

"I don't know about that," I pipe up.

"No?"

"You miss the final experience that way," I say. "It's what you're building up to seventy or eighty years; seems a shame to miss it."

I notice Jenny, her gaze shifting between us like she can't believe what she's hearing. She raps heavily on the side of her own head. "Hellooo," she yodels. "Am I really hearing this?"

Mandy looks at me imploringly. *Change sides*, the glance begs. *Don't be her accomplice.* And what really hurts is that's exactly what I'd like to do: I'd like to help Mandy out. I'd like to wear a different uniform for once, be the good guy instead of the sidekick. In my head I hear Jenny saying, *I do it all for you, you know.* Back in The Parrot, when I thought the boots would come at us any minute, it was sweet and pathetic and frightening all at the same time. And when Jenny called about the pitbulls, got that guy all riled up, I hated it but I wanted it to go on. The experience as drug trip. It all seemed defensible somehow. But this time it's different. Here in Zellers, surrounded by cheap women's underwear and a pretty store clerk. I used to be absolutely solid in my support, but suddenly the sweetness has gone. It seems so desperate, her need to put one over on the world. It's not who she is, or used to be. It sure as hell isn't who I am. My patience is spent. If I were Mandy I'd tell her to take a hike; I'd laugh in her face.

I keep formulating and reformulating my mutiny, hoping vainly that, at the umpteenth repetition, the order will be reversed one more time and Jenny will come out on top.

But nothing changes. And so I betray her. I wait for Mandy's attention to flit my way again — it does quickly, as if she's expecting me to produce a gun or a note demanding the impossible — and then I roll my eyes, a *Can you believe it?* sort of gesture.

Jenny still has her back to me. "Maybe it's the weave," she

says. "Maybe, you know, the setting on the factory loom, or weaver, whatever machine it is they use, maybe it was set at too high a tension. It's like stringing a tennis racket, right?"

"That sounds unlikely," Mandy says. She has seen and assimilated my gesture. This has moved way past the point where she needs to see a proof of purchase. She moves a little closer to Jenny. Only a few inches but enough. Subliminal *Jeopardy* again. "Perhaps you made a mistake. Is that possible?" Mandy says, trying to give Jenny a way out. "I'd hate to take this any further if it might end up causing some..."

"Some what?" Jenny bellows.

I lean forwards and half-whisper, "Embarrassment."

"What?"

"Embarrassment," I say again. Then: "She knows."

"Who knows?"

"Mandy."

"Who the hell is Mandy?" Jenny says, not looking at me, just receiving my voice in her ear like a misdirected phone call from the other side of the world, still fixed on the store clerk.

"I am," Mandy says simply. She picks up the pink sweater she discarded earlier. She lifts a knee and uses her thigh as a surface on which to fold the arms into the back. The shocking pink and the raised leg make me think of a flamingo.

Jenny grabs my arm. "What did you do?"

I shrug, catch myself looking at Mandy the exact way she was regarding me. But to expect her help is ludicrous. She has no investment here.

"You gave me up?" Jenny says incredulously, an inch from my mouth. Close enough to kiss or bite. Mandy, in a display of decency, moves off a couple of steps, pretends not to be watching.

"Don't you think she knew?" I mutter. "It was too far-fetched, this one. A loom wound too tight? I mean really. Circulation cut off completely. Come on, Jenny. You're hung over. You still reek of Cuervo, for Christ's sake."

"She was going for it. The game was still in its early stages,"

Jenny says. "So fuck you." She rams a finger into my breastbone.

I look at her puzzled. Jenny points the finger at Mandy, who is smiling uncertainly. She really is a dead ringer for my cousin. And I think, maybe that's it: she seems like family.

"And you too," Jenny says to her. "I should smack that pretty face of yours."

I move between the two of them, a reluctant referee. "Come on, Jenny."

Mandy looks about warily. In the distance a willowy man appears. He's in his fifties, tweed jacket and scarlet bow tie, his hair combed over. He hovers an aisle away. A man looking for a fox hunt, I think. And, as if reading my mind, Jenny begins imitating the call of a bugle or a trumpet; at any rate she creates a strange discordant music deep in her throat.

Then she stops abruptly and snaps, "Wait in the car."

"I don't get it," I say.

"You didn't want any part of this. You said so earlier. I should have listened to you." She wraps one leg of the nylons around each fist. The crotch droops between her hands. She pulls the whole lot over her head. The legs hang down like great rabbit ears. She growls at us, feral, and I try to decide if she's really lost it or whether this is part of the show, the grand shoot-em-up before the credits roll.

"Jenny..." I start, but I can see this isn't going to have a happy ending. "I didn't mean..."

"Go!" she blurts, pulling the stockings from her head as if it's a final act of defiance, like the bank robber who has decided there's no tomorrow. Static electricity causes Jenny's hair to stand up wildly. She looks mad. "Sayonara," she says, waving as if I'm a mile away. "Toodle-loo."

It's the wrong thing to do, I know, but I take her cue and walk away. Half-way through Toys I turn and see her in animated conversation with Mandy and the man in the bow tie. The man looks confused, as if a life spent unpacking work boots and ogling lumpy cashiers has rendered him unfit for this sort of chaos. I feel a twinge of regret. Jenny would have had a field day with a guy like that. Perhaps if she had gone for him instead of Mandy I would have laughed my way through it. Maybe she would have pulled it off.

I sit in the car for maybe twenty minutes. Deciding to go back for her, then deciding to drive away. Back and forth. A plain woman in an outlandishly short dress scoots by with a plastic bag full of water and one angel fish. You can tell she is trying hard to keep the water calm: her lips are pursed and she seems almost to glide over the paved lot. An old man with red suspenders arcing over an enormous belly coaxes a young boy into the back of an old Buick. But it's not at all sinister. His grandson, probably. Off for a barbecue. Or to read from a favourite book. Silly stuff. I check my face in the rear-view, interested to see whether my own sudden garish sentimentality has got me blushing. I crave tequila, the sharp crust of salt on my lips.

And God knows what state Jenny has worked herself into by now. I worry about her. Never seen a woman capable of such instant passion, willing to argue all day for a lost cause. It's never enough to simply sit back and take it in. I muse on that a while. Just general *What makes someone tick?* stuff, nothing concrete or profound. And then, unexpectedly, something resolves for me. It's not like a camera shifting into focus, or a bathtub epiphany, merely the muddy, messy sense that I've got it all wrong. I've been too close to the action and needed some widescreen distance. And from this relatively safe vantage point — hands on the wheel, key in the ignition — I appreciate for maybe the first time that Jenny is, even now, providing a dozen people, strangers, with something to talk about over dinner. A respite from the dreariness of back-to-school routines, all that greeting-card bull. *I saw the wildest thing today,* they'll say over their pork chops, their apple sauce. *This woman, you should have seen what she did. She had these stockings ...*

I check out my bleary visage again, then take in with some sadness the empty seat beside me. It's wrong, this absence of Jenny. Even as I think it I know I'm the corniest guy alive, and that tomorrow it'll be bleak and anxious for me again. But hey, face it, I'm the getaway driver. The sidekick. Not that I'm a fatalist, not by a long stretch, but that is how it shapes up for me. Which at the moment is perfectly fine.

I gallop back across the parking-lot — too aware of myself, how I must look a lot like a loosed ape, vaguely dangerous — and I push in through the revolving door. Past the thirty foot waterfall, the pink granite cliffs, and back into Zellers.

At first I can't find Jenny. Then I glimpse Mandy, wrestling with a lime green windbreaker behind the Customer Service desk. She senses trouble, I think, and tries to duck around the corner. Normally that would be enough to discourage me. Now, though, propelled by a different fuel, something akin to certainty, I smack down hard on the dainty silver bell perched atop the Formica.

"Mandy," I call, and she pokes her head out nervously. "Which way?" I point to the left and right as if that might help.

"Security office," Mandy says sheepishly. "She was making quite a fuss." She shrugs into her jacket and fumbles with the zipper.

"It's still a bit warm for that," I say, wanting (without knowing why) the upper hand with this pretty girl I betrayed Jenny for.

Mandy smiles weakly, a skim-milk sort of smile. "Probably not," she says. Then, "It's down that way."

I head along the wall. Grebs stacked head-high on three racks. Reeboks next, then cheap tea-baggish brogues and furry slippers the colours of popsicles and sprouting tumorous animal heads from the toes. Tigers, zebras, elephants, rabbits. Then it's Jenny behind glass in a white, low-ceilinged office. She sits uncomfortably on a wooden chair that looks too small for a child. Behind a steel-legged desk is the bow tie man. And standing to Jenny's left is a minimum-wage security guard, arms crossed as if he's a bit player in a made-for-TV movie.

I try the door handle. It's locked, so I drum on the glass, politely. Jenny sticks out her tongue, glares insolently, like I'm the chief of police, the boss of these interrogators. I grin foolishly, all teeth and scrunched-up red eyes, the picture of awkwardness and delight. I lean on the window ledge and begin to laugh; it bubbles, boils out of me. I gesture at the security guard to open the door and he checks back of the desk for guidance. Bow Tie holds up a finger, mouths *Just a second*, and turns to Jenny, asks her a question. I rap more insistently on the glass, ticked off at his nerve. Jenny, for the first time since we got in the car a few hours ago, tips her head back and laughs. It is strange to see the sound but not hear it. The laughter registers nevertheless as a vibration in my head, my gut, as if a nebulous string of atoms connects the two regions and the gesture plays me like a guitar.

Bow Tie continues to ignore me and I look around for I don't know what. I pick a pair of size eight tigers off the rack and launch them into Home Furnishings. Jenny, predictably, applauds. She puts two fingers in her mouth and creates a whistle so piercing that the top end makes it clear through the glass. The security guard practices his stoicism, and Bow Tie looks flustered. I pick up elephants and decide to air them out. I hurl the pachyderms towards the escalator. Joe Montana, I think. Steve Young on a good day. They land on the top metal step and are carried smoothly downstairs towards Tupperware, Curtains and Carpets. "See the world, ladies," I say.

It looks like things are turning ugly. I see the security guard whip out a walkie talkie and grumble into it. Almost immediately a similar navy uniform, ill-fitting and shiny, is bustling towards me past a long line of attentive turquoise vacuum cleaners. I point him out to Jenny, who has stood up now. For some reason I had assumed she wouldn't be allowed to make that move. I guess I'd imagined myself part of a John Le Carré piece, or Len Deighton, a mall crisis much more sinister.

"Run," Jenny yells.

I don't hear her but I see the word take shape in her mouth. It floats forcefully and hits the glass. And so I run. I grab an armful of slippers and take off. The Security Office door is flung open behind me and the guard barrels out. Two of them on my tail. Beautiful. Then Jenny appears. She makes a break for it, dashes headlong at the long line of tellers. Bow Tie pursues her but looks instantly winded, his knees seem not to bend properly as he lurches across the floor like a poorly articulated puppet. Because we're a team, me and Jenny, I fastball a pair of tigers at her and she leaps them easily, a gazelle too fleet of foot to be hunted down. I make it into the mall proper and it's packed, an absolute cinch for me to disappear. And anyway, the security guards stop at the metal barricade like it's a state line, a border crossing and the limit of their jurisdiction.

I catch my breath at the bank machine. A kid in line behind me — reflective shades and a Metallica T-shirt — puts his hands on his hips and spits into the corner. I shake my head but stop short of mouthing off at him. I take out twenty bucks and zip next door, pick out a nice bottle of chardonnay. It's the right wine and I'm pleased with myself. Because something a bit civilized seems in order. We'll have a quiet night, I think, as I stroll back into the crowd, letting it carry me along at its own pace. Rent a movie maybe. Something with Meg Ryan in it. We both like her, though probably for different reasons.

I get out to the parking lot and Jenny's already waiting in the car. Window rolled down, feet up on the dash. And what feet. Twin and pristine fuzzy tigers, still joined together with a nylon price tag.

"Try walking in those," I say, on top of the world. Jenny catches wind of my good spirits, sees the wine, and her face lights up. She doesn't have anything smart to say, but that smile, just like I knew it would, fills me with the energy of a hundred suns when I climb in beside her and turn the key.

Weird

Suddenly everyone in the room is talking about books. Who they like to read, who they're reading at the moment, plot lines, crises, how money spent on a book is money well-spent. So I leave my coffee behind, get the hell out, even though my last two bucks paid for those couple ounces espresso, that twist of lemon. In *Sea of Love* all the crooks are sent invitations to a party with the New York Yankees. When they show up with their baseballs, their eight-by-ten glossies, their starry-eyed kids, Al Pacino busts in, cracking his cop smile, walking on air.

Some things are too good to be true, that's the message I'm getting.

And now, other end of town in the deadest bar I can find, chipped pool balls glowing unearthly and randomly over the green velvet, I'm still uneasy. Not a soul in the place but I'm looking over my shoulder anyway, waiting for the wrong door to open. The bartender's thumbing through a mystery, and a sweaty young Hemingway is spearing marlin over the urinals. This place could be part of it too, I swear.

This afternoon? The whole world's gone weird.